'Touch me and tell me that there is nothing at all left between us.'

Eleanor held her fists tight against her skirt. 'The pull of flesh is only a fleeting thing. Honour and trust and duty are the tenets that a sensible woman lives by.'

'And you are sensible?'

'Very.' The word was as forceful as she could make it, moulded by her depth of fear.

Unexpectedly Cristo smiled and took three steps back. 'Logic and reason run a poor second to the heat of passion. Should you relax your guard for a moment, the truth of all you deny might be a revelation to you.'

Pursing her lips, she allowed him no leeway. 'My life has changed completely since Paris, and I am a woman who learns well from her mistakes.'

'Mistakes?' He echoed the word, turning it on his tongue as if trying to understand the very nature of its meaning before finding a retort. 'I have relegated our night together to neither blunder nor error. Indeed, I might have chanced something entirely different.'

AUTHOR NOTE

The Wellingham brothers rule Society with their wealth, titles and intellect.

You met Asher, the Duke of Carisbrook, in HIGH SEAS TO HIGH SOCIETY, and Lord Taris Wellingham in ONE UNASHAMED NIGHT.

Now it's Cristo's turn—the youngest brother and the most mysterious.

Returning to London after many lonely years in Paris, Cristo Wellingham, the Comte de Caviglione, meets the one woman he never expected to see again—a woman ruined by the dark secrets in his past.

ONE ILLICIT NIGHT

Sophia James

First published in Great Britain 2011
Harlequin Mills & Boon Limited,
Eton House, 18-24 Paradise Road, Richmond, Surrey TW9 1SR

© Sophia James 2011

ISBN: 978 0 263 21819 0

Harlequin Mills & Boon policy is to use papers that are natural, renewable and recyclable products and made from wood grown in sustainable forests. The logging and manufacturing process conform to the legal environmental regulations of the country of origin.

Printed and bound in Great Britain
by CPI Antony Rowe, Chippenham, Wiltshire

This book is dedicated to
Frances Housden and Barbara Clendon
for their help with my writing.

Sophia James lives in Chelsea Bay on Auckland New Zealand's North Shore, with her husband, who is an artist, and her three children. She spends her morning teaching adults English at the local Migrant School, and writes in the afternoon. Sophia has a degree in English and History from Auckland University, and believes her love of writing was formed reading Georgette Heyer with her twin sister at her grandmother's house.

Previous novels by the same author:

FALLEN ANGEL
ASHBLANE'S LADY
HIGH SEAS TO HIGH SOCIETY
MASQUERADING MISTRESS
KNIGHT OF GRACE
  (published as THE BORDER LORD
  in North America)

MISTLETOE MAGIC
  (part of *Christmas Betrothals*)
ONE UNASHAMED NIGHT

ONE ILLICIT NIGHT
features characters you will have met in
HIGH SEAS TO HIGH SOCIETY and
ONE UNASHAMED NIGHT.

Chapter One

Château Giraudon, Montmarte, Paris—early November 1825

Lady Eleanor Jane Bracewell-Lowen could not quite focus on the form of the man who carried her, could not through the dizzy grey fog of lethargy see the expressions on his face or hear the cadence of his words. With a growing dread she tried to shift her weight so that he might let her down, let her escape, but even that was impossible. Nothing on her body worked and the tight mesh of the heavy wig she wore brought a strange dislocation.

She was naked! She knew that, for she had felt his hands on the curve of her breasts and in the warmth beneath her legs. Rough. Lewd. She could not even turn away in protection. Nay, sheer apathy held her caught against breath that smelt of hard liquor and bad teeth.

'You're too beautiful for *une pute*. When you finish here we'll treat you well below.'

Une pute? A whore? Two words that did make sense.

Eleanor closed her eyes against the horror of truth, this small movement all she could muster as shock made the hairs on her arms stand out straight against the chill of the night.

'I…am…not a…whore.' The sounds came out as only nonsense, no meaning in them as she failed to form the letters on her lips, just gibberish, fear making her feel sick.

A door opened and warmth beckoned. Beyond the darkness in a circle of light, a solitary figure sat at his desk writing.

'Monsieur Beraud sends you a gift, Comte de Caviglione.'

She stiffened. The man she had come to see! Perhaps he would help her. If only she could speak clearly…

Silence was the only response.

'He said that she was new to the game.'

At this the man in the shadows stood. Tall and blond, the expression on his face matched exactly the wariness of his words. His eyes were the deepest of brown.

'Did you search her for weapons?'

'I did much more than that, *oui*.'

In one movement the blanket was gone and Eleanor was set down on to a bed.

'*Merde!*' The tall man's curse was rough. 'You stripped her?'

'In readiness, you understand. It's rumoured to have been a while since you last had a woman and it's my master's view that the bile of celibacy can make any man cantankerous.'

Dark eyes wandered across her own and Eleanor failed to summon the energy to protest.

'A whore who even now readies herself for your use, *mon*

Comte, though if you do not want the gift, I could take her below…'

'No, leave her.' The blond man raised his hand, a flash of heavy gold rings caught in the light, the expression on his face guarded.

She tried to blink, tried to warn him, tried in the singular and only way that she could to alert him to the wrongness in all of this, but the second was gone as he looked away, his hair falling across his face as he turned.

Beautiful. At least he was that. Closing her eyes, she was lost into the ether of nothingness.

Cristo Wellingham waited until the minion of Beraud had gone before crossing the room to slide the heavy slats of oak into place.

He had never trusted locks, for a soul well versed in the art of picking them could take but a moment to force his way through any door. Neither did he trust the fact that Etienne Beraud had sent this whore to him as a gift. The man was a scoundrel and a cheat working for the French police in a way that was blatantly illicit and this 'offering' was undoubtedly another of his attempts to gain favour and benefit from the world surrounding the Château Giraudon.

Looking down at the girl, Cristo doubted that she was as inexperienced as Beraud claimed her to be, with her plumped-up lips and overdone face powders. She smelt of cheap drink and old perfume, the sort that was sold in the markets on a Monday where the Boulevard de Clichy crossed into the Place de Blanche.

Still to give Beraud some due, she was indeed striking,

though he doubted the overlong blonde curls to be her own, wound as they were around her hips and catching the firelight in a way that seemed patently false.

Tweaking a single lock, he let it fall across her ample breasts with their pale pink nipples and a smattering of freckles.

Freckles. God. Swiping his hair, Cristo moved back, afraid suddenly of the immensity of desire that ran through him. Beraud had his reasons in trying to sweeten a deal between them, he supposed, for the wide and varied circle of acquaintances flowing through the château represented a great cross section of Paris society, making any gathering of information infinitely easier.

The girl moved, her hair falling from the line of her breast, and his body tightened unbidden. He loosened the folds of fabric around himself. Already the small whistles of slumber came from her breathing, the sleep he had seen in her blue eyes taken with all the speed of one who was not quite… cognisant.

Drugs? Or wine? With the telltale odour of alcohol on her breath he determined it to be the latter. Brandy, probably, and a dosage that was far too high for a woman so slight. If she died here…?

His fingers closed around one shapely calf and he shook her awake, pleased when her eyes opened again.

'What's your name?' He didn't particularly want to know it, but if he kept her talking she might give him some clue as to Beraud's intentions, and with the way Fouche's forays into politics were shaping up that could be more than useful.

The candlelight reflected in her pale eyes and she remained silent.

Sensual. Worldly. A voluptuous and erotic token from a man used to blackmailing and bribing his way into power. Why here and now? His mind ticked over the timing as he tried to determine what Beraud might gain tonight in his desire to have her in this room with him. The codes he had been working on were close to being finished. Had the French police some word of that? Even a glance from a practised eye might unearth secrets that would be better hidden and Cristo was well experienced in the fact that spies were most efficient when their form was unexpected.

The clock on the mantel chimed the hour of eleven and downstairs in the salons another bout of debauchery was in full flight. There were sounds of women laughing, a bottle being de-corked and the louder chants of men made loose with sex and spirits.

Once he would have been amongst them, taking his chances with courtesans who welcomed his attentions. But he hadn't for an age now, the ease of orgasm no longer an opiate for what his life had become.

The girl before him moved suddenly, her scent potent, and his fingers dropped away. She was young to be so very badly used and Beraud's taste in the intimate arts had never been simple. Two marks on her left thigh caught his attention, the burn of raised blisters sitting strangely against alabaster skin. When he leant forwards to touch the wounds she did not flinch, but watched him under languidly hooded lids.

'Combien as tu bu, mon amour?'

How much did you drink, my love?

A murmur he could not fathom was her only answer as she turned to him, a come-hither look in the way her limbs fell loose accompanied by the heavy smell of her perfume. The powder she wore smeared beige across the white of his clean linen sheets. He hated the way his hand would not obey his mind and pull away, the heat of her quiet seduction a narcotic without rival, the contrived 'little girl' look a decided bonus in her line of work.

Lord. If he could have imagined a woman to ignite his fancy she would indeed have been the one lying naked and available on the bed before him.

He should leave her, should walk away and order her removed, but he found that he could not. It was the feel of her skin that pulled him closer and the shape of her hips tapering down to long and damned fine legs.

Tight bound in a growing need, one finger nudged all that was hidden and he smiled as her head arched back against the pillow. A courtesan of some skill, he determined, as her muscles coiled, tighter than a whore should ever be and her breath no longer steady. With a care that surprised him he began to stroke, wanting her pleasure to match his and their coupling to resemble something far from the quick and lurid encounter that Beraud probably had in mind. As he closed his eyes against the cosmetic accoutrements of her trade and the falseness of the wig, it was easy to imagine other things—things that were true and right and good, the world that had been his once, before his sins had changed it.

Shaking his head, he came back into the moment, years of living in Paris concentrated in his hands, fondling with pressure and rhythm, asking for response, his breath blowing cold across heat, tightening her womanhood and raising her hips.

Something was happening to her, some dreadful, exquisite, carnal thing. No longer could she lie there wooden and tense when every fibre in her body ached with a feeling of thick want.

Wrong. It was all wrong, but a stronger force now propelled her.

Farther. She wanted him to move in her farther and she could not stop the groan that left her lips or the throb-beat of her skin around the gentle warmth of his fingers. A maestro. Playing her. Taking the rigidity of fear and replacing it with a loose and easy longing. Everything. Nothing held back. Hard against soft. Surrender.

'Shh.' He tried to hold her still, but she would not be calmed, his fingers lending panic to the edge of her need.

Don't stop.

Don't leave.

Closing her eyes, she concentrated on the feeling that had scattered all other thoughts aside, reaching for the craving that bore her down hard against the mattress even as his clever hands squeezed the very life from honour.

He felt her come, felt the muscles close against him rigid, thick in ecstasy, her sigh all that remained of breath. Spent and replete!

His whore now. God, Beraud had the measure of him after all, Cristo thought, as he unlaced his breeches and readied himself to mount her. Her wetness beckoned, the solace of women inciting a particular appetite in him that could no longer be denied. Straddling her open thighs, he positioned himself above, parting the soft lips of her core and fitting them around his heavy thickness.

The warmth of her crept into his soul as he thrust in hard to be confronted by the one barrier he had never expected to feel there.

Virgin?

The thought was as fleeting as the breakage and the giving and his full, tight engorgement. He could not have stopped himself even had he wanted to and the seed that he seldom left in any woman spilled warm against her womb, the last whimpering of his cock a question of flesh against better judgement.

A virgin whore. A trick. His mind sharpened as he lifted himself off her, the liquid of sex on her skin.

She had turned away from him now, eyes closed against seeing, languid abandon reforming itself into a tight kind of anger that he recognised. The corruption of innocence made him swear.

Who the hell was she? Who the hell had done this? To him? To her? The look in her eyes, as he had demanded a name and the incoherent reply—asking for help?

Lord above. He had been in the game of intelligence for years now and he had missed that? Real regret surfaced and guilt that held consent sacred in any relationship. He had never been a man to use force with a woman and virginity was something to be protected and given with full knowledge. He swore again, hating Beraud anew for sending him a brandy-filled whore-virgin completely new to the game.

More questions surfaced as her medallion suddenly glinted against the pillow, the long gold necklace no longer hidden by her blonde curls. Removing it from her throat, he took it into the light and knew that the past had found him.

Tricked. Duped. Another link in the chain that bound him here, lost to the pathways of proper society and for ever shamed.

Eleanor felt a rush of imbalance engulf her. Her palms fanned wider against the whiteness beneath and she struggled to find reality.

Naked. She was naked, though such a consideration was nothing against the sudden and dreadful knowledge of what had happened. Keeping her eyes shut tightly, she wished she were dead.

'I know you to be awake.' In French.

She turned her head, even as she knew she meant not to.

'Why do you wear this?'

He sat in a chair with his long legs stretched out in front of him and her grandfather's medallion dangling from his fingers, the lines drawn in gold catching the candlelight and sending rainbows spinning across the ceiling. His breeches were loose and his shirt was unbuttoned at the front, the breadth and definition of his chest so remarkably foreign that she could not look away.

Parts of the last hour were coming back. A great rush of redness covered her cheeks, though when his eyes passed across the juncture at her thighs she understood that what motivated him now was only anger.

'Who the hell are you?'

When he reached out to press the heel of his hand hard against her stomach she was mortified by the tight need that echoed from the gesture.

A whore. He had made her such! The play of his fingers against her skin made her stretch towards him, every sinew wanting…

His palm broke contact.

'For a woman without experience you are surprisingly wanton.'

Eleanor turned her head. Below the shouts of people became louder, glass falling against a harder surface and shattering from the clumsiness of inebriation.

A brothel.

She was in a brothel on the bed of a man whose very den of iniquity it was. Deflowered.

She smiled at such a term and then felt a single tear trace its way down her cheek to be soaked up by the burgundy velvet in the pillow behind. His string of French curses told her that he had seen it too.

Lady Eleanor Bracewell-Lowen? England and the rarefied world of the *ton* seemed a long, long way from here.

Chapter Two

Cristo held the medallion in his fingers and hated the fear in her face.

'Who are you?' he repeated, his voice not quite steady. He wished he might have left her there, just walked out into the night and waited until she had gone, but life was no longer that simple for him. Beraud had brought her to him and if the woman should know anything of his past, what then? For years he had held the secrets safe. He shook his head, hard. With her maidenhead lost he felt he owed her at least something.

One moment ran into two and then five more. But still she did not speak and the heat of fury leaked out of his vengeance.

Sitting back, he weighed up the options.

She would not talk and he no longer felt the desire to make her. She was shivering, too, for the fire had long since died out, as the cold of an early Parisian November crept into the space of his chamber, raising the fine hairs on her arms.

He caught at an eiderdown of goose feathers folded on

a chest at the foot of the bed and placed it across her and when one foot was still exposed he was careful to tuck it into warmness.

The first stirring of dawn was lighting the room and the bells of Sacré Coeur rang in those souls who still believed in the goodness of Our Lady. Striking a light, he breathed in the mellow taste of a cheroot, the smoke winding its way up through the lonely morning dark, another small reminder of all that he had become.

'*Mon Dieu, et quel bordel tout ceci.*'

My God, and what a hell of a mess all this is.

He saw small toes wiggle free from the thick down covering as she tried to sit up.

'Could I please have a drink?'

Six words that nearly undid him, for the quiet dignity in her request was undeniable. When he filled a glass and handed it to her she made a point of saying thank you, though the realisation that he still could not place her French accent kept him edgy.

'How came you here?'

She remained quiet, but as the flints of blame in pale eyes continued to prick at his conscience he made an attempt at explanation.

'I didn't know that you had not lain with a man before. This is a place that never shelters innocents and by the time I found out that you were one, it was too late.'

An apology of sorts. It was all he could manage.

'Then you will let me go now, *monsieur*?'

Turning his face towards the window, Cristo wished that he could have taken her from this room right then and there before the need his body shook with was too much to deny. But he could not, for the party below was far from over and men made careless from too much drink were always dangerous.

A temptress. A siren. The full line of her lips and the rise of her ample breasts against the softness of the cover. The sheer need of her made his voice sharper than he intended.

'Where are your clothes?'

'Downstairs. I took a drink…more than one.'

'You came in with the other women, *les prostituées*?'

She nodded.

'And the chain?'

'My aunt was once given it by an English client she serviced. A bauble that was not to her taste! I liked the shape and she said that if I came with her tonight I might have it, should the evening prove a success…'

'Your aunt is one of those below?'

When she nodded his hand closed around the engraved coat of arms and he felt the edge of the rondel dig into his palm. Was such a coincidence even possible? With a lifetime of deception behind him he knew that it was seldom the case. Could he make her talk now that she was more sober? His world reformed into only suspicion and his heart began to thump as he wondered how much Beraud might have gleaned about the meaning behind the crest.

Keep talking, Eleanor thought to herself, the fog of the drink she had been forced into taking receding into the sharper play for survival. Already the velvet darkness in his eyes looked harder, more removed. Just a whore plying her trade in a market driven by a commodity that could be given many times, the first of as little importance as the hundredth. She had to make him trust exactly that if she had any chance at all of escaping with her name intact.

'I do not believe anything you have told me. Do you work for Beraud?'

'Beraud?'

'From the Parisian Police. The man who sent you to my room.'

'I do not know the man. I came with my aunt and—'

He stopped her simply by raising a hand. 'You lie, *mademoiselle*, and I intend to find out why.'

Her laugh was harsh as she bit back a reply, but he no longer seemed interested, the drag of his chair shrill against the parquet flooring as he stood and walked towards the windows.

'Perhaps you would prefer to join the others downstairs and further your trade? You could no doubt turn a trick or two with the one who brought you in here. He certainly looked willing enough.'

True fear squeezed the very beat out of her heart. 'Oh, I think I would rather stay with you, *monsieur*.'

His smile held no humour whatsoever. 'Take care, *ma chérie*, of expressing any such yearning, for there are many in this game who would not give you the luxury of choice.'

Her hands fisted beneath the soft warmth of down. *As you gave me no choice.* She almost said it. Almost let the scalding shame escape, but didn't, as sense embedded itself into silence.

Ruined.

The very word was written in her blood on the sheets, and the laughter from below seemed only to emphasise the silence between them, making everything more awkward again. She saw him pick up a tumbler and then place it down, undrunk, and the swell of the vessel was engraved with a crest.

Isobel had warned her of the intemperance of men such as this one when she had first arrived in Paris, but her friend's timely cautions had been buried by need. Her grandfather had instructed her to make certain that she delivered a letter into exactly the right hands.

'Le Comte de Caviglione at the Château Giraudon. Give this letter only to him, Lainie,' he had said time and time again as life had left him. 'Only to him. On your oath, promise me that you will do this, for he is a good man, a man to be trusted and he needs to know the truth.'

How naïve she had been to imagine she could just walk up to the door of the Château Giraudon and demand the ear of its master or expect the dignity and decorum that honourable men in the courts of England might have afforded her. Her dress had been a little gaudy, but the wig was an expensive one she had procured before leaving London. Perhaps it had been the presence of the women installed there already, their brightly coloured gowns and heaving bosoms giving an illusion of something that was normal here in Paris.

It had taken less than an hour for those downstairs to ply

her with too much brandy as she had waited, trying not to appear as nervous as she felt.

Lord, if the Comte had come earlier she would have placed the missive in his hands and left as she intended: a dutiful granddaughter undertaking a final wish for a beloved grandfather. But now? She dared do nothing else to raise this man's suspicions with all that lay between them, for if he ever guessed her name…

Against the breaking light Eleanor could see his profile. He was almost as young as she was and for that at least she was thankful.

'Where are you from?'

His words held distrust and the caution of one used to betrayal. She noticed the small finger on his right hand was missing altogether as he laid his palm against his thigh.

'Do you speak English?' He had switched languages now and his accent was pure aristocracy. The change made her tense as layers of mystery clouded truth. Who was he? Why had he asked her that? She swallowed before she answered.

'*Pardon*, *monsieur*, I do not understand what you are saying.' She tried with all her might to make her words sound the same as one of the maids at Bornehaven, the soft Provençal French easy to mimic. The lines of his shoulders relaxed.

'The south is a long way from the streets of Paris, *ma petite*. If you need money to return there…?' He switched easily to French.

She shook her head. Payment could only mean obligation

and with nothing to trade save her body, she was careful. He took the words a different way completely.

'Then if you are hell-bent on staying in the city, perhaps you and I could come to some agreement.' The fire in his eyes was searing sharp.

Eleanor pressed back against the bed, watching as he came closer. 'Agreement?'

'Your line of work is somewhat…insecure. I could offer you a less uncertain future.'

'Uncertain?'

He began to laugh, his teeth white against the dawn, and in that moment Eleanor knew the pull of beauty, fierce and undeniable, his eyes marked with arrogance and temperance and authority. Not a man to be trifled with. But it was the hint of something else that held her still. A sadness, she thought, written beneath a careful detachment.

He stopped as he reached her and ran his thumb along her cheek. Without force. A bolt of awareness sizzled between them, making her heart beat faster.

'Though if you truly wish me to halt, *mademoiselle*, then I will.'

He meant it. Honour came in unexpected places, she thought as she caught the depth of his dark, dark eyes, and the silence between them lengthened.

She should pull back, should shake her head and put an end to it all, but she was held immobile, her nipples tightening and the want in her belly finding a home in the place between her legs.

Le Comte de Caviglione! Her grandfather had said he

was a good man, a trustworthy man, a man with some tie
to the Duke of Carisbrook…

One time or ten more, what did it matter when the urgency
in her being called only for release and already the damage
was done, was it not? The pressing insistence of some emotion that was uncontrollable made her turn to him!

She did not flinch when he rolled down the cover and
exposed her breasts, cold tightening desire and adding to
the allure of surrender.

The velvet counterpane was burgundy, and stitched in
gaudy golden thread. She felt the ridges of it against her feet
when his hand ran across her throat and made them stiffen.
Above the bed a net of gauze was anchored by ribbon, the
cane hoop that held it painted in an antique peeling silver,
so that the colour bled into the fabric. Beyond that, a mirror
was fastened to the ceiling, catching the movement of them
both through a veil of muslin, the pale outline of her breasts
surprisingly wanton.

The reflection of the man beside her with his night-black
eyes and magnetism left her little chance of refusal. The
length of his hair fell past his shoulders, pale spun silver as
she reached up to touch the colour.

He smiled, his glance allowing no modesty, and the distant sounds of a waking Paris were a counterpoint against
her growing need.

'How old are you?'

'Eighteen.'

He turned her leg into the light. 'What happened?'

The rings of blistering skin on her thigh stung as he
touched it. 'I tried to keep my gown on.'

'Modesty in a whore is unusual.'

'It was cold...'

He laughed this time and the sound was freeing, no longer caught up in control. Reaching for a drawer beside the bed, he removed a tin of salve, wiping the ointment on carefully, lessening the pain. When he had finished, he did not break contact, but spread her legs. The soft flesh throbbed in anticipation.

'How much were you paid?' The question was almost a caress.

She remained silent, the scale of payment for a lady of the night so far from her knowledge.

'I'll triple it.'

'And if I refuse?'

'You won't.'

A loud burst of shouting below made her start.

'The party will not be over for a few hours yet,' he added as his fingers left her skin. 'And the minions of Beraud are restless. Make your choice, *ma petite.*'

She caught his hand and held it, slender and elegant, the nails trimmed and clean.

'Then I am at your service, *monseigneur.*' She had heard the other women downstairs use this phrase in the salons of the Château Giraudon. In the playing of a part came safety and she ran her tongue around her lips in the same way those below had mastered, slowly, and looked straight at him.

His eyes were a thousand times older than his face, the chocolate melted into harder shards of amber. Danger and distance and steely control, the fickle carelessness of youth constrained by another menace. But she took a chance on those eyes and those hands and on the words of a man who had not excused the actions of one who had hurt her.

'Instead of payment I would ask of you a promise.'

He was listening, the stillness in him haunting.

'A promise that come daylight proper you will spirit me out of this place in your carriage and let me go wherever I should will it without question!'

She was relieved when he nodded.

'Is it just Paris you would escape, *mademoiselle*, or might I hope that the perils of the night have started to sink in?'

She only smiled as he peeled away the cover, a few feathers of down escaping the velvet, and one fluttering into the air to land on her stomach, white softness caught in a greying morning. He leant across and blew it away, the warmth tickling her skin and making her breath just stop. Her head arched into the pillow as a quick stab of passion lanced through her, the blood beating in her temples like a band, the base of sound blotting out everything save the sensation of want wound tightly through every pore on her skin.

He laughed. 'Perhaps, *ma petite*, I do you a disservice after all, by letting you leave Paris and a profession that seems your milieu.' He held the hardness in her still with his hands and waited till the shafts of need had passed before discarding the bedcovering altogether.

He should never have called her bluff, Cristo thought, but her words allowing him everything were a powerful aphrodisiac.

I am at your service, monseigneur.

God, he was twenty-three and hardly a saint, and if the

Devil were to smite him into Hell for such an act then he was willing to take his chances. One time more or many, her virginity was already lost. The tremor in her hand as she had held it up to demand his promise to let her go free only added to his intemperance, and the way she looked him straight in the eyes saw to the rest. He was primed and ready, rock-hard with desire, the outline of his manhood raising the fabric of his breeches in a way that was…unseemingly desperate.

He wished he might have hidden it, hidden this power she had over his body, but he could not and would not and as the clock struck seven he realised that the morning was being eaten away and that his promise of freedom was close.

'What is your name?'

Suddenly he wanted some truth. Something more than falseness and business.

'Jeanne.'

She whispered the sound so that he had to strain to hear it. Jeanne?

He wrote the letters on her stomach with his tongue and traced the word again with his fingers, lightly. All the hairs on her right arm rose, the colour nowhere near as pale as her tresses. Almost dark. Her nipples budded into knots as he skimmed his touch across them and the heartbeat in her throat beat blue against the last smattering of summer freckles.

So delicate and breakable and so very fragile; just a girl on the edge of womanhood. His hand wandered downwards to feel the wetness, slick, tight and heated.

He moved then to the softness of her thighs and to the

rounded shape of her hips, skirting the outline, making her know in his exploration how truly beautiful she was. Not just a whore. Not just a night or a coin. No contract in any of it save desire.

Her lips parted and her breathing quickened as his touch moved back to her centre and then away at the very last moment so that he did not quite fulfil her hidden want. But he felt it. Felt it in the way her skin rose against his hand, swollen with need.

Sweat beaded her upper lip and her forehead where her fringe had fallen. He knew that heat, too, in the place beneath his cheek as he bent to the juncture of her thighs.

This time she did shout out, shock resonating as his tongue reached in, tasting the fine wine of woman, and her hands threaded in his hair like an anchor, keeping him caught, as the flame does the moth.

The fire of youth and sex and passion. The lust of a hundred days of abstinence and many years of caution. The memory of what it was like once to only feel free. He drank like a man newly come from the desert until all that was left was her.

Her skin. Her smell. The feel of her fingers in his hair, holding him closer.

'Jeanne.' He moved back as he said her name and when no flicker of recognition passed into her summer-blue eyes he knew even that was a lie.

Still, he could not care. She was here and he was here and her blood on his sheets more real than any falsehood could ever be.

He moulded the swell of her breast into the palm of his

hand and lifted the softness. Full fat abundance fell across the space between his first finger and his thumb. No little girl here. Her chest rose, fast and then faster.

Bringing her face to his, he opened her mouth to a kiss, surprising himself by the want, and when her resistance faltered all he knew was bliss. Her tongue, her cheeks, her face in his hands turning to him, the pull of knowledge, the sharp tang of certainty, the urge to own and keep and possess.

When he unlaced his breeches and lifted her onto his lap she did not fight him, and when she felt the tip of his sex pause for a second before pressing inwards, she welcomed the deep ache of it as her head lolled upon his shoulder. Submitting. Yielding. Nothing essential save the heavy rigidness of his manhood felt in the core of her body.

'Ahh, sweetheart,' he said, dampness on his forehead as her breasts fell heavy between them. Eleanor revelled in his expertise, in his finesse, in the way he built her hunger along with his own 'til there was nowhere for either of them to go. Except up and away into the realms of fantasy and delight, and the sheer relief of orgasm.

He held her afterwards this time, against his chest, stroking her back with his fingers as the noises of the traffic outside became louder. His shirt of the finest linen was damp in sweat and she wondered why he had not discarded it, the smell of musk and man embedded in the fabric. Perhaps it was because of the scars she had felt raised upon his back when her fingers had lingered there?

Caught in a world with no one else near, she became

braver and leant over to trace her tongue around the shape
of his ear exactly as he had done to hers.

His breath simply stopped and the scent between them
was pungent and insistent, another binding that held them,
another sense fuelled by wonderment.

Cristo let her take him this time, his control slipping into
an unfamiliar acquiescence. He liked the way she held him
tentatively, with the palm of one hand splayed against his
chest and the hard length of his manhood pressing deep into
her stomach.

When the other fingers curled around his shaft he tensed
and she pulled away, until his fingers again found hers and returned them, the pure uncertainty leaving him breathless.

He wanted to move, wanted to topple her beneath him, but
she held him with her fingers, her breasts grazing his chest
and the length of her false hair tying him to immobility.

'God, help me.' His voice sounded nothing like it usually
did and this time he spoke in English, a sure sign of just
how far his restraint had slipped. Turning, his body covered
hers, heavy and true, as he drove in hard because there was
no moderation left in him, no restraint or inhibition. The
shuddering finality of his release brought him a liberation
he had long thought of as past.

'God.' His voice was not kind as he slipped from her
a good twenty minutes later and crossed the room to the
privacy of his bath chamber, the oath repeated again as he
comprended the full enormity of what had just happened.

Beraud's purchased whore was making him care again, feel again, hope again.

Laying his forehead against the cool silver mirror, he closed his eyes. The girl was dangerous with her alabaster skin and her elemental sensuality. In his world, anything of value was a way of losing control, the weakness of concern an easy weapon for those who would want to harm him. And there were so many who did!

He needed to have her gone before others sensed an attachment and used her innocence as a pawn, needed to protect her in the only way that he still could.

Pulling on his breeches and finding another shirt, he walked back into the room, the anger marking his movements with haste.

Chapter Three

Eleanor could barely understand all that had just happened.

Now he looked angry, unemotional, a different shirt buttoned full around his neck. No longer biddable. His hair was tied tightly into a queue and slid down the silk on his shoulders, an overlord of the dark underbelly of Paris, the four fingers still left on his right hand all bejewelled.

A stranger, only that, no vestige left of the lost hours shared between them. No remnant of a softer man who might truly cherish her. Just danger and hazard and difference, and a choice of life that showed in the hard lines of his body and face.

Eighteen and set apart from everything now, a fallen woman, a stupid woman, a woman who would never again quite fit in to the strictly governed world of her upbringing. Spoiled goods. What husband should want her?

Her breath came quick and shallow as she fought back the pooling tears!

* * *

She was going to cry now, he could see that in the way she tipped her head down and dropped her shoulders. A girl who had made a choice she regretted, her deep red lipstick smudged across her mouth like a wound.

'Where are your clothes?' He made no effort at all to moderate his voice.

'Downstairs in a b-b-blue chamber, but my gown was badly torn.' Fright had made her shake, the cover she was draped in shivering with some force. Excusing himself for a moment he unfastened the slats on the door and asked a servant to find her attire.

Then, moving to his wardrobe, he found a woollen jacket and a satin skirt that some woman had left here a few months back. 'Put these on for now.'

She reached out for them and he added a scarf of fine wool from the many lined up at the back of his closet, noticing the feminine way she fashioned it around her neck. Her long wig was caught up in the heaviness of the layers and he saw darker locks below. All a ruse?

Interest sharpened. 'How well do you know Beraud?'

'He is one of my aunt's clients.'

'Then if you know what is good for you, *ma chérie*, you will stay away from him. His tastes run to the more eclectic...' He tapered off, tired of trying to warn her, tired of taking responsibility for a whore who knew exactly what it was she was doing.

He could not save them all. He had learned that truth years ago when the first woman to plead for assistance had spent his gold on a bottle of the finest cognac and thrown herself off the bridge of the Pont d'Alma. Her body had been dragged up with his engraved watch in her hands and the weight of the law had descended, demanding answers that brought him notice he was far from wanting. Since then he had been much more careful.

He looked away as she stood and dressed, the slight reflection of her outline all that was left to him in the window. Even that he eschewed for the view outside, the first stirrings of the carriages and people in the vicinity of the Rue Pigalle.

Dislocated. One word rent from all that he so usually kept hidden, the sheer and utter waste of life and goodness and innocence slapped against a harder, more selfish world.

His world! Falder Castle glimmered like a golden promise on the edge of memory, the endless waves of Return Home Bay calling out in a hollow chant, *'Come back, come back, come back.'*

But he couldn't, not ever, the consequences of sins binding him to the necessity of distance.

Shaking his head, he refused to think about the past and as he caught Jeanne's measured glance he made himself relax.

A layer of tragedy coated her seducer's night-dark eyes. Eleanor saw it even as he smiled and the core of her anger melted just a fraction. He was beautiful. She doubted she had ever seen a more beautiful man, even with his overlong hair and clothes that would not be out of place in a theatrical production in the West End of London. As she looked around, the room gave the impression of a faded glory, the strips of silk and velvet on his bed mirrored in the heavy curtains and ornate corded ties at the double-sashed windows. A piano of considerable proportion stood against the farthest wall, sheet music draped across the top. Books stacked in piles on the floor completed the tableau, the titles in an equal measure of both French and English.

With clothes on she felt braver, standing to run her fingers across the spines. Not lightweight reading, either. Moving then to the piano, she pressed down on a note of ivory, the sound echoing around the room in perfect pitch.

A well-used and well-maintained piano by Stein. She read the make in the words above the keyboard. The frothy, vivid orange skirt she wore swung out from her legs as she turned, surprising her with its easy movement—the sort of garment a dancer might use or a courtesan? With no undergarments the satin was cold against her bottom.

A short rap on the door took all her attention and with surprise she saw the man who entered was dressed exactly as her own grandfather's butler might have been at the turn of the century.

'Milord.' His accent was pure Northern England! 'The carriage is readied.'

Carriage? She could go? Now? Le Comte de Caviglione would keep his promise free of question and all consequence? Or was she to be taken somewhere else?

'I would thank you for keeping your word, sir...'

She broke off when a bejewelled hand was raised, as if her appreciation was of absolutely no interest to him.

'Are these items yours?' He gestured towards a serving

girl who had walked in behind the old man carrying her cape, boots, hat and purse.

A great wave of redness surged into Eleanor's face as all attention settled upon her, for, with the tumbled bed linen and the scent of brandy and sex, the room held no mystery as to what had happened there. Servants talked with as much fervour and detail as did any daily broadsheet and the contents of her bag would give extra clues again.

Could she even begin to hope that the letter was still inside? That the promise she had given to her grandfather might still be honoured?

The older servant stepped forwards with her possessions. 'These items were left in the blue salon, *mademoiselle.*'

'Thank you.' Reaching up, Eleanor fastened her hat. With no mirror the task was more difficult than she had anticipated and the wig made it harder again. Still, with a bonnet in place and the warm cape around her shoulders, hiding the mismatched assortment of articles beneath, Eleanor felt... braver. She pulled on her boots in less than a moment and, pretending to pick up something off the floor, extracted the letter as the Comte conversed with his man.

'Milne will see you into a carriage. The driver has been instructed to take you where you would wish to be set down.'

Hardly daring to believe that the promise of freedom was so very close, she followed the old man out even as the Comte de Caviglione turned towards the window, dismissing her in the way of a man who, after using a whore for a night, is pleased to see the back of her come the morning.

Tucking her grandfather's sealed envelope into the folds

of the tumbled sheets as she passed the bed, she saw that the dawning sun had bathed the Comte's hair in silver.

Cristo watched as the carriage pulled away on the driveway below, the white pebbles caught in the eddy of the wheels reminding him of another place, another home and far from here.

His hands fisted at his sides and emptiness was a taste in his mouth, sour and lonely. He longed for a greener land and a house that sat in the cleft of a hill with oaks at its back and roses in the gardens.

Falder.

The name echoed in the corners of regret; shaking his head, he turned to the hearth, leaning down for the kindling in a box near the fire. The simple task of catching sparks calmed him, made the fear he could feel rolling in his stomach more distant.

When he had finished he reached for the leather pouch in the hidden drawer of his armoire and sent the previous week by The Committee.

Secrets helped. Codes demanded single-mindedness and logic, searching for a pattern amongst the random lines of alphabet and numbers. Conradus's book and Scovell's principles made it easy and his interest quickened. His cipher wheel sat on the desk at hand.

Hours lay before him to be used up in concentration and attention. No sleep. No dreams. No lying in the grey of morning and wondering how the hell he had come to such a pass.

The bold scent of the girl lingered though, distracting

him. Making him hungry. Again. For her warmth and the feel of flesh. Unspoiled.

He picked up his pen and dipped the quill into ink, blotting it before setting the nib onto paper. Her locket lay on the table before him, the chain of gold thin and delicate. He remembered the look of it around her neck, fragile and pale, the skin almost translucent.

He traced the certain shape of it in his mind. There had been a time when he had not known anything of dying and killing, a time when the sound of death had been impossible to describe. He could not lie to himself that those who had met their Maker because of him all had perished for the greater good or for the Golden Rule. Intelligence was a game that changed as the seasons did, and greed had as much sway as loyalty. To king or to country.

Not to family. He had long since been cured of that.

The columns on his desk refocused. Page seventy-five, column C, the fourth word down. A message began to form in the mass of chaos, though a capital letter threw him. The calibration had been changed and then changed again, the common combinations no longer locked into pattern. Transposing always had a point, though, and he looked for a letter that appeared the most frequently.

R. He had it. Substituted for an E. Now he just had to find the system.

He had been eighteen when he had started out on the dangerous road of espionage. A boy disenchanted with his family and alone at Cambridge. Easy pickings for Sir Roderick Smitherton, a professor who had been supplying the cream of the latest crop of undergraduates for years to the Foreign Office; Cristo had topped the new intake in every subject, his skill at languages sealing the bargain.

When he started it had been like a game, the Power Politics of Europe under the fear-spell of the memory of Napoleon, a man who had won an empire by his skill of manoeuvre.

Cristo had arrived in Paris the son of a Frenchwoman and the bequest of her château had given him a place to live. His father's liaison and his mother's shame had had a few points to recommend it, at least, and he had set up a spy ring that worked inside a restless Paris where priests and prostitutes had become the mainstay of his intelligence.

He liked the hunt, those few hours that came between months of blinding boredom, for in them he found forgetfulness of everything, his life held in a reckless balance that was only the responsibility of others.

Pull the trigger and end it all.

He wondered at the resilience of the human condition every time his hands reached their own conclusion and reacted, the whirr of a bullet or the sharp, quick pull of a knife. Often in the moonlight and in the hidden corners of this city in spaces where people held secrets that might bring down a nation by a whisper of breath or a clink of coinage. Always counting. Not the lives that might fall on the toss of a dice or the shake of a head. Not that. Counting only the cost of what it took to stay in the game and one step ahead. And alive!

He pulled out a cheroot from the silver tin he kept in his top drawer and tapped the end against the fine mahogany of his desk. Wrong and right depended on one's point of view, though he suspected that his own moral compass had long since been tarnished by expediency, and the misguided idea that he might have once made a difference was only a distant memory in the dark labyrinth that was his life.

The code before him blurred into nothingness and he stood and crossed to the window.

His carriage had not yet returned and he wondered where it was that 'Jeanne' had wanted to be taken. He should have gone, of course, just to make certain that she arrived safely and that the destination was noted.

'Mon Dieu!' The words were loud against the silence and his breath frosted the glass. With an unusual sense of poignancy he wrote a *J* in the mist and rubbed it out just as quickly, the regret in him surfacing.

He could find her again. Or he could lose her for ever, in the wilderness of mirrors and shadows where nothing was fixed.

Only grand deception and infinite loneliness—and if prostitution was the oldest profession in the world then surely the business of spying must have come in a close second.

Too close for comfort were he to reconnect with a woman who might mean something!

He watched as a few of the prostitutes walked from his house to be swallowed up by the traffic in the street, their gaudy nightdresses as out of place as a peacock in a farm-yard barn. He hoped that one of them was Jeanne's aunt and that something she had told him was true. Perhaps then they would laugh together about the night over a cup of tea and plan the evening's frivolity.

The thought annoyed him, but he had no dominion over

his little whore's body and to demand so would only be foolish. Still, the anger would not dissipate. Nor the want. His eyes strayed to the bed trussed up into disarray, the cover that had warmed her tangled into many folds, the tail of it sweeping the floor. Empty.

Only the smell of her perfume remained, heavy in the air with the tang of alcohol! He drew in a breath to keep her closer and then stopped.

No. Jeanne's association with Beraud could only be dangerous for them both. Reaching for the tumbled sheets, he tossed them into the blazing fire at his hearth and watched as linen caught flame. Better to leave her in memory. Delightful. Innocent. Always young. He only wished that he had known her name.

Dropping the medallion into a box of oddments in the bottom drawer of his desk, he had resolved to put her from his mind when his glance was caught by parchment flaring brighter than fabric.

A letter. He could see the scrawled writing on the burning envelope was addressed to him. Quickly he reached for the brass poker and extracted the remnants, stamping on the flames as they refused to die.

Only a few words remained on the sheet inside but they made his heart slow. *Nigel. Murdered. Blame.*

No coincidence at all then, but the beginning of blackmail. Turning to the wall beside him, he punched his fist hard against it until every knuckle bled.

Chapter Four

London—June 1830

Martin Westbury, the Earl of Dromorne, laid his newspaper down and looked across at his wife.

'Now here is an interesting snippet, Eleanor. It seems the youngest Wellingham brother has returned from the Continent bearing both fortune and a foreign title to reside in London. They say he is looking for a home in the country. Perhaps he might find The Hall in Woburn to his liking? That is a property that might well suit such a man.'

Eleanor considered her husband's query. 'I know only a little about the Wellinghams. Is the family seat near there?'

'No, indeed not, for Falder Castle lies in Essex. I am surprised he would not acquire property around those parts instead. He runs bloodstock, according to the paper, and is quite an expert on the choosing of prime horse flesh.'

The sounds of laughter interrupted their conversation as Martin's nieces Margaret and Sophie came into the room.

At seventeen and eighteen respectively they presented a picture of understated beauty, their gowns of matching yellow sprigged muslin floating in the breezy warmth of a new summer's day. Their month-long sojourn in London with their mother, Diana, had made them full of energy.

'We had a wonderful time last night at the Brownes' ball.' Sophie's voice held such an edge of excitement that Eleanor was instantly curious. Looking across at her husband, she smiled.

'Cristo Wellingham is the most handsome man to ever grace London, I swear it, and he dresses in clothes that have come straight from Paris. Did you ever meet him when you were there all those years ago, Lainie? I doubt that you could have missed him.'

Eleanor froze, the lost night in the winter of 1825 leaving her momentarily speechless.

'Oh, she was far too busy with me, Sophie.' Martin easily deflected the conversation and pretended to look more than hurt when the girls laughed.

'We know that you are her heart's desire, Uncle Martin,' Margaret teased, 'but can't a girl at least look?'

Leaning over, Eleanor took her husband's hand in her own, liking the warmth and familiarity. 'Your nieces are young and frivolous and their shallow measure of a man's worth is a testimony to that fact.'

'How cruel you are, Lainie.' Sophie's tone was soft. 'But your insult must also apply to the other young ladies who were at the Brownes' last night.'

'When is this demigod next in circulation?' Martin's question was threaded with humour.

'Tonight. There is a large gathering at the Theatre Royal Haymarket. A comedy by James Planché is showing and it is supposed to be very good.'

'Perhaps we should go?' Martin's voice sounded stronger than it had in a while, but Eleanor began to shake her head, a vague disquiet building behind her smile. Something was wrong, she was sure of it, and yet she could not put her finger on just exactly what it was.

'Please, Eleanor. It has been ages since we all went out and if Martin feels up to it?'

'Of course! Our box has been severely neglected of late, and I am sure your mother would also enjoy the outing, Sophie.'

Cristo watched the rain from the window of his house overlooking Hyde Park. Summer rain slanting across the green grass blurred the paths that crossed the common.

He lifted the brandy he had brought with him from Paris and took a liberal swig straight from the bottle. His brothers would be here soon and he would need all the succour he could muster. He wished he could have cared less than he did about what it was they might say to him, but the wildness of his youth had alienated him entirely and they had probably been as happy as his father to know he was leaving England. His father's first letter to find him when he eventually reached Paris had made certain he understood that returning to the family fold was not an option. The memory still hurt, but he shoved it aside. He could help none of it and what was done, was done.

Only masquerade. Only deception. England and its airs and expectations made him take another good mouthful of brandy and then another. He should not have come back, but ten years on foreign soil felt like a lifetime and the soft green heart of England had called to him even in his dreams.

'Would you be wanting your black cloak, or your dark blue one this evening, my lord?'

Milne, his butler, held a cape on either arm.

'The black, I think. And don't wait up for me tonight, for I shall be late.'

'You said the same yesterday, my lord. And the night before that.'

Cristo smiled. Milne's frailty worried him, but the old man had too much pride to just take the substantial amount of money that Cristo had tried to give him and retire. Paris had aged him, too. Just one more blame resting upon his shoulders with the shady dealings in the Château Giraudon, sordid repayment for Milne's devotion and loyalty and belief. In him. It was a relief to leave it all behind.

'My brothers should be here within the hour. If you could show them up.'

'Yes, my lord.'

'And if you could ask the housekeeper to prepare tea.'

'Yes, my lord.'

He placed the bottle of brandy on his desk inside a cabinet and closed the doors. Alcohol was one of the factors in his lengthy estrangement and he did not wish for the evidence to be anywhere on show. Tea seemed an acceptable substitute.

The cravat at his throat felt as restrictive as the dark blue waistcoat lying over his crisp white shirt and the new tight boots hurt his heels.

'Asher Wellingham, the Duke of Carisbrook, my lord,' Milne announced, 'and his brother, Lord Taris Wellingham.'

Cristo stood as the two men walked into the room, a scar that ran under Taris's left eye giving the first cause for concern, though Cristo showed no evidence of it as he waited for speech. Asher and Taris looked older and harder. Neither smiled.

'So you *are* back.' Ashe had never been a man to beat around the bush.

'It seems that I am.' Cristo didn't care for the cautiousness he heard so plainly in his words, but the distance between them was measured in a lot more than the few feet of his library floor.

'You have blatantly ignored our many efforts to stay in touch with you,' Ashe reminded him. 'Over the years the notes you sent back indicated you held no fondness at all for the name of Wellingham or indeed for us. Yet here you are.' Each word held a sharp undercurrent of blame.

'Are you well?' Taris spoke now, a note in the question that unexpectedly tipped Cristo off balance.

'Very.' Even in the many skirmishes of Paris his heart had not beaten so fast.

Asher looked around the room, taking in the lack of ornamentation, he supposed. Or of belongings! Taris's glance, on the other hand, never wavered once.

'Alice always hoped you would return.' Ashe again. The barb tore at Cristo's composure and he looked away.

Alice! The only mother he had ever known. Damn them. He felt the hand in his pocket grip the skin on his thigh. Damn England and damn family. Damn the hope that had never been extinguished, even in the most terrible of times.

'As it seems you are here to stay, I have arranged your introduction back into society and the family fold in the guise of a theatre visit. With a lot of darkness and distraction we should at least look as if we enjoy being a family and if this is going to work at all, appearances matter.'

Ashe's irony was so very easily heard.

Cristo nodded, not trusting himself with more. He had left England vowing never to return, his wild ways at Cambridge inflaming loyalties and stretching the already-frayed love of his family. He had never fitted in, never dovetailed into the strict and rigid codes his father had laid down and when everything had finally unravelled after Nigel Bracewell-Lowen had died in the cemetery in the village near his home, Cristo's father had been the first to tell him that he was not a true Wellingham, or a legitimate son of Falder.

Cristo swallowed back the bile of remembrance as he remembered his father's final tirade. Ashborne had dallied with a French woman on his travels, a small meaningless tryst he had said that was 'ill-advised, wrong-headed, inappropriate and more than foolish'. The words still had the power to hurt even all these years later, for what did one say to a parent so condemning of his very conception and of the woman who had birthed him?

The other side of the coin had also held damage. Alice, his stepmother, had taken him in at Falder and loved him like her own and if a whisper of his true parentage was ever mentioned he had not heard of it. The three-month-old Cristo de Caviglione had become a Wellingham, his name written into the family Bible by Alice's very hand. She had told him that much later when the tensions between him and his father had resulted in the truth being thrown in his face and she had hurried to London to plead with Cristo to stay.

Love and anger entwined in deceit, and now a different duplicity. Cristo hated the beaded sweat on his upper lip as his oldest brother outlined his plans for the evening.

'Our wives shall also be accompanying us to the theatre.' The tone Asher used was so very English.

Emerald Seaton and Beatrice-Maude Bassingstoke! Cristo had kept up with the family gossip while in Paris and the two women were by all accounts as formidable as his brothers. He wished suddenly that he might have had a formidable woman at his side, too, dismissing the thought with a shake of his head.

'There are bridges to cross if you are to gain acceptance here, given the wild ways of your youth and of your questionable exploits in Paris.' Taris tilted his eyebrows in a way that gave the impression of searching.

'I quite understand,' Cristo answered quickly. A public place would ensure distance and formality, the baser emotions of blame and redress submerged beneath the need for 'face'. Years and years of an upbringing that revered the word 'proper' would at least see to that. It was a relief.

The tea that his housekeeper bustled in with seemed a long way from the good idea that he had initially thought it, and her rosy smiling face was the antithesis of all expressions in the library.

When she left he was glad, the plumes of steam from the teapot and the three china cups and saucers beside it little harbingers of a life that he had left and lost, a very long time ago.

Ashe was already showing signs of retreat. 'Then we will see you tonight.'

'You will.'

'At half-past seven.'

'On the dot.'

Taris raised the black ebony cane he held towards the teapot. The dimpled silver ball on the end of it glimmered in the light. 'I'd like a cup.'

'It's tea, Taris.' Ashe's explanation was given quietly.

'I know.'

'You don't damn well drink the stuff.'

Cristo watched as Taris brought out a hip flask from his jacket pocket and unscrewed the top. 'I just asked for a cup.'

Merde. Cristo remembered his brothers' banter with an ache. Many years younger, he had never really been a part of such repartee, no matter how much he had wanted it.

Reopening the cupboard door, he raised two crystal glasses from the green baize beside a new bottle and placed the lot down before them. 'Help yourselves.'

'You won't join us?' Ashe again.

'I try to ration myself these days.'

'Ashborne would be pleased to know of it.'

The mention of their father fell bitter between them, the past knitting uneasily into a growing silence.

'I doubt he would care much either way, actually.'

His meaning settled on his brothers' faces as a question and he wished he might have taken such bitterness back, the sheer anger in his words giving away much more than he had wanted.

'Perhaps you did not know that he left this world calling your name?' Ashe's expression held all the indignation that his ducal title afforded him.

'A death-bed wish for clemency is such an easy request given he could barely stand my company in life.' Cristo had recovered his equilibrium, though Taris began to speak with a great deal of emotion.

'With the reputation you have garnered in Paris, perhaps he was right to send you away. The Carisbrook title is an old and venerable one after all, and it needs each and every one of us who bear it to bring it proudly through the next decades.'

An argument that might hold more weight were I a true Wellingham.

Cristo almost said it, almost blurted the sentence out with little thought for consequence, raw anger still holding the power to hurt. But the memory of Alice stopped him.

Better to smile, the illusion of a family tied in blood and ancestry and one unbroken line of history more palatable than the other face. His brothers' dark hair shone in the lamplight, like a stamp of belonging, or a badge of title. So very simple if you only knew where to look! His own reflection in the polished mirror made him turn away, the silvered fairness belonging to a different lineage altogether.

Gulping back the last of his brandy Taris poured himself another, the clock on the mantel chiming the hour of three. 'So you are home for good, then?'

'It's my plan.'

'How did you lose your finger?' Ashe's interest was almost dispassionate—a conversation topic as mundane as the weather or the happenings at the last ball.

'On a ship after leaving England. My opponent came off worse.'

'Rumour has it that a good many of your opponents have "come off worse," as you put it.'

'Rumour is inclined to favour exaggeration.'

'One false step back here and society will crucify you.' Asher's voice held a hard edge of warning. 'In Paris the extremes of human behaviour might well be tolerated. Here you won't have that luxury, and I won't stand idly by and watch you squander the Wellingham name. Neither will Taris.'

Now they were coming to it. No more vague innuendo or ill-defined familial congeniality. His careless past had caught up with him and the gloves were off.

'I did not come home for that.'

'Then why did you come?'

For a moment Cristo thought to lie. To merely smile through it all, and just lie, but here in the heart of England he found that he could not.

'I came back in order to live.'

Neither of his brothers answered him and he felt the muscle along the side of his jaw ripple as he held his silence.

'God.' Ashe swore and then swore again as the sun broke through the clouds outside, flooding the room with light. Taris looked up into it, holding his left hand to his face in a peculiar movement, the line of his fingers open to the warmth.

'Lucinda sends you her love,' he said as he lowered his arm.

His sister.

'Did she marry?'

'No. She is adamant about remaining a spinster.'

'Quite a choice.'

'The same could be said of your preferences.'

Ashe collected his gloves and hat from the chair beside him and Cristo stood when they did, pleased that in the years between then and now that he had grown a good two inches taller than either of them. He shook their hands as a stranger might, vaguely aware of the crest of the Carisbrooks engraved into the heavy gold of his oldest brother's ducal ring.

'We will see you this evening, then.'

'Indeed.'

He watched as they followed Milne out of the room and when the door shut sat on the arm of the sofa and balanced there, neither standing nor sitting. The day darkened as he continued to look out of the window, listening to the bells of some church mark off the hours and the occasional shout of English voices from the streets outside.

Home.

The smell of it all was different. Softer. Greener. Known.

I came back in order to live! The idea of it spun untrammelled in the corners of his memory and the secrets that he held marked his heart with blackness.

Chapter Five

Eleanor did not wish to go out that night; the wind had heightened, tossing the clouds around the sky, and a homely fire in the front parlour beckoned.

Still, with the arrangements made and Sophie and Margaret speaking of nothing else all afternoon, she felt trapped into it.

The gown she wore was of sapphire-blue silk, the pelisse having a chenille fringe skirt and a ruffled underskirt in cream. She had had the dress made the previous summer, but the style had not yet slipped from fashion and she enjoyed wearing the garment. On her wrist she wore a pearl bracelet and at her neck a matching strand that had been her mother's. Her hair had been fashioned with corkscrewed curls around her face, the length braided and pinned at the back.

All in all she thought she looked passable, the colour of her eyes deepened by the shade in the dress, though the same disquiet that had visited her earlier had returned again.

She breathed out hard, chastising herself for worrying.

She was twenty-three years old and the catastrophe that might have been her life had settled into a pattern that was… comfortable. Her family was safe and happy, she kept good health and lived in a discreet neighbourhood.

She needed nothing more, so when the tiny worm of denial flared she stomped on it hard. *'Nothing,'* she said and made certain that she had change in her reticule and a handkerchief should she need it before leaving the quiet of her chamber to join the others downstairs.

Cristo walked into the Theatre Royal Haymarket, late. He had missed the first gathering, he knew, but Milne had caught his foot on a corner of the carpet and the physician had been called to make certain that nothing was broken.

One night, he thought, to scotch the rumours of a Wellingham family feud and then that would be the end to it. One night to mingle and smile and then he would be left alone to pursue what it was he needed from England.

Peace.

Solitude.

A place to breathe without the fear of a knife in his back or a secret around the next corner!

As he pushed aside the curtains of the family box, the darkness kept him still whilst his eyes became accustomed to the lack of light. After a moment he could see his brothers and the seat they had left between them.

For him.

He slipped in without apology and acknowledged Asher to his left. Three women sat in a tight row in front, one dark-haired, one blonde and one… Lucinda. She turned to gaze at him with eyes that had not changed one bit in ten years and blew him a kiss.

He could not help but smile at her *joie de vivre*.

Across the theatre in the boxes at the same level he saw others watching, their eyes barely glancing at the comedy on the stage. Below, too, a good deal of the patrons looked up.

The prodigal son or the black sheep? Cristo was pleased Milne had made such a fuss with his clothes, the frock and waistcoat he wore of the highest quality. Criticise me at your peril, they seemed to say, and as he adjusted his cravat he caught the eye of the dark-haired woman sitting directly in front of Taris. She did not smile or move, yet he felt a rapport that was unmistakable. Beatrice-Maude Wellingham, his middle brother's wife. A woman of substance and intelligence and pure, clear wit! He had read her writings in the *London Home* and admired her views. She looked away as he failed to and he felt himself tense. When the lights came up again for the interval, he was pleased to stand and stretch.

Lucinda, his sister, was the first at his side.

'You are long overdue, Cristo, and it is said that you are looking for a place to stand your bevy of bloodstock. I have heard that the Graveson property is on the market for the first time in a century. Perhaps that would do.'

He had forgotten the way she approached things so directly, though interest was piqued as she mentioned the land that stood on the Falder boundary. He wished that his brothers had told him of it, but dismissed the chagrin quickly for the tall woman with turquoise eyes had come to stand beside him and she took all of his attention. When Ashe moved towards them Cristo surmised her to be his wife, Emerald Wellingham.

She did not introduce herself, but took his hand into her own and held it. The silence lengthened.

'My brother might appreciate his hand back, Emmie.'

'Well, he cannot have it just yet, my love, for I am not quite finished.' With a jolt Cristo realised that she was reading his palm.

'Long life, great wealth and fine bloodstock?' he quipped as she remained silent.

'And the unexpected end to a journey,' she added finally, closing his fingers and letting go.

'She has a great gift for it.' The dark-haired woman joined them, Taris at her side, one arm threaded through hers. 'And if I could give you a word of warning, it might be that Emerald's predictions are never wrong.'

'Indeed, it must take great skill to deduct that I have just travelled back to England.' The sarcasm in his voice was not becoming, but he had had dealings with others reading his fate and none had come anywhere near close to his demons.

'It is not that journey I am speaking of,' Asher's wife added. 'There is a woman who was important once…?' Her eyes bored into his and for a moment Cristo felt almost light-headed. He was glad when Lucy pushed between them, voicing her wish to stretch her legs.

Eleanor thought the play was lovely and yet the feeling of tension seemed magnified with each passing moment of the interval. Standing with Martin's nieces and his sister Diana, taking in the cooler air of the lobby, the pillar behind her was a welcome place to lean against.

She felt scared. The word surprised her. Scared? Of what? Inherent suspicions ruffled the hairs on her arms and neck. Margaret beside her suddenly stood on tiptoes, peering towards the other end of the room.

'There he is! I knew that he would come tonight.'

When Eleanor made no effort to look, Sophie nudged her forcibly. 'The youngest Wellingham brother, Lainie. The one we told you about.'

The crowd before them thinned a little as people moved forwards and in the space that was left she saw the back of a tall blond man, his hair caught in a short queue at his nape.

All breath left her body. There was something about the shape of his head and the colour of his hair and the tall strength of him—something familiar.

No. No. No. Don't let it be him!

He began to turn, smiling at the fair woman on his arm, and his dark eyes came up to her own, falling through the distance to a château in Paris, naked, brandy-soused and ruined. The lamplights blurred and the floor, once solid beneath her feet, began to sway, dizzy arcs of denial and horror and something else that she could never have admitted.

She was glad to feel Diana's hand beneath her elbow as her knees simply gave way, and the floor was cold beneath her face.

Stark and utter disbelief kept Cristo still as he tried to make sense of what had just happened. His virgin whore from the Château Giraudon was here, dressed in deep blue finery, her hair pinned in a series of elaborate loops and knots, the blonde wig she had worn in Paris hiding a treasure of russet, chestnut and chocolate.

'My God, it is Eleanor Westbury, Emerald.' Beatrice-Maude's voice was concerned. 'She has fainted. Where is her husband?'

Husband? The world began to get stranger as Cristo stopped the urge to simply move forwards and pick her up in his arms, the paleness in her face obscured now by others who had hurried to her side.

A sofa behind them proved to be a godsend and a young man Cristo presumed to be the one Beatrice-Maude spoke of bent down and lifted her onto it. Flashes of sapphire blue could be seen between the forms of concerned helpers as a doctor from the crowd kneeled down with a bag of physician's tools.

Within a moment Cristo saw consciousness return and she tried to sit up, the uncertainty in her movements as she swiped away her hair transporting him back to his room at the Château Giraudon. He swallowed and heard a question directed at him. By Asher's wife, he determined, and there was more than the normal quotient of curiosity in her voice.

'Pardon?' He was dazed, caught in the quandary of choice. The woman they named Eleanor Westbury had not tried to find him again with her glance, but had kept her eyes carefully downwards, her small hands wringing the fabric in her copious skirt, and the line of her bodice heaving with breath that was too uncertain.

The muscles of her femininity coiled around his fingers, the scent of sex and release and want and the naked glory of her body unresisting and easy.

Shaking with the effort of remaining so still, Cristo was wary as the glance of Emerald Wellingham met his in question.

'Do you know her?'

He shook his head, not risking speech, and listened as Beatrice-Maude related to Taris exactly what was happening in a low monologue.

Why would she do that when the scene was right in front of him?

Another truth hit him as he turned: because his brother could not see any of it. When he looked to Ashe for the clarification of what he suspected, his oldest brother nodded. Almost imperceptibly.

The world turned on its axis, skewered by time and knowledge, no little truths these. No tiny unimportant discoveries.

The French whore who had been brought naked and willing to his bed was none other than a married English lady of the very first order and his brother Taris was blind.

'Here is Martin Westbury, the Earl of Dromorne, now.' Emerald spoke again and with interest Cristo sought out the man she had identified.

He watched as Eleanor's husband, old and grey and confined to a chair, was wheeled to her side, watched how her fingers curled into his when he came there, the affection evident in such an action making him turn away.

'That is Lord Dromorne?' His question was blurted out

with little finesse. The man looked as though he should be in a sanatorium somewhere, the colour of his skin a pallid grey.

Emerald nodded. 'Yes, and it is rather a love match, for he is very wealthy and simply dotes upon her.'

So Eleanor Westbury was a woman with a position to keep up in society? A well-heeled and well-brought-up lady, according to all he had heard of her, and one who had no place at all being in the backstreets of Paris's night-time debauchery.

He was glad when the chimes sounded for patrons to return to their seats as it gave him a chance of escape and to mull over all that he had learned.

Would her illness be serious? Had she seen him?

A thousand questions turned in his head and yet in the midst of shock and disbelief another truth began to fester.

He wanted to see her again, wanted it with a desperation that made his breath shallow with aching.

'I am all right now. Truly, Martin, I am all right. I do not know what came over me. Perhaps it was the closeness of the air or something that disagreed with me at dinner.'

Her husband had made so much of her swoon that Eleanor just wished he might take her words as truth and leave the matter alone. The Comte de Caviglione! Cristo Wellingham was the Comte de Caviglione with his velvet bed and his gauze-covered mirrors.

'But you are always so strong. I have never before seen you so much as cry—?' He stopped.

Eleanor squeezed his hand as much in gratitude as in

shock. Tucked up in her bedroom, with soft down pillows at her back and a fire lit to banish the slight chill of an early summer evening, everything was in its place. Normal. Usual. She did not even dare to think about what might happen tomorrow.

For tonight she was safe. Home. She pressed down the guilt of five long years.

Come the morning there might be other topics that raged in the drawing rooms of London's elite. Stories of ruin and stupidity. Cautionary tales about how the foolish ways of young women could so easily lead to the demise of reputation.

Letting go of her breath carefully, she answered her husband's questions in the manner of one who only had small worries to consider and was glad when he finally kissed her on her forehead and left for repose in his own sleeping chamber.

When the door shut behind him she blew out the candles on her nightstand and slipped out of bed, opening the curtains and the window to let in the moonlight and the breeze. She felt freer in the darkness than she had done all day and was glad for the cool air above the heat of the fire. Martin felt the cold in a way that she never had, immobility adding to the problems he suffered with his circulation.

Her brow was clammy and sticky, the revelations of the evening leaving peril and fear as a crawling shock across her skin.

Cristo, the third son of the late Duke of Carisbrook was le Comte de Caviglione?

Had he seen her? Would he remember? His hair was

shorter than it had been in Paris and his clothes were very different. But the sheer force of him was exactly the same: magnetic, dangerous, menacing. He looked like the panther she had seen in onyx a few months before in a little antique shop off Regent Street. Ranging across its territory, marking it out. Fine linen and wool did not disguise any of Cristo Wellingham's contours or dull the measure in his glance. When her eyes fell on the charcoal portrait next to her bed, the risk of all she loved, all she held dear, was heightened again.

Florencia: her pale hair silvered and her cheekbones falling in exactly the same line as her father's.

A letter came for her the next morning.

It was not monogrammed, so she was unprepared for the missive. This time, however, she was alone in the quiet of her room, the pile of mail brought in by her maid and deposited in the silver platter on her desk.

Cristo Wellingham's handwriting was just as she would have expected it to be, boldly fashioned in capitals and in ink that was the colour of the midnight sky in high summer.

He wanted to see her when she could find the time. Just that! There was no explanation of why or where or how. Her feeling of dread doubled at the thought of refusal. If she did, what could be the consequences? Would he blackmail her, bully her into paying for his silence, or might he demand some service...again? For the second time in under twelve hours she felt the breathless terror of vulnerability.

She could, of course, tell no one. Martin hadn't a notion as to Wellingham's other identity and no other soul save

Isobel, her friend in Paris, knew the real truth about her missing months in France. She shook her head and banished the worry. So far this morning there had not been a whisper about the reasons for her ridiculous faint at the theatre last night.

This was something that she had to face alone. But where could they safely meet? What possible destination would hide them from others, but be public enough to protect her? She needed an urban location, she knew that, but the parks were too crowded.

She also needed a destination that she might walk to, for her demands of a carriage made ready for her sole use would only incite curiosity given that she seldom ventured anywhere alone.

The thought made her start. Once she had been brave and free and adventurous, any challenge taken on with relish and delight. Like the delivery of her grandfather's letter! She winced at the memory and pushed the thought aside, her eyes straying to the pile of books beside her bed from Hookham's Lending Library in Bond Street.

A library. The spacious and elegant area of the place was public enough to be safe without being overfilled and they could repair to the assembly rooms on the first floor if there should happen to be anyone she recognised. There were chairs in the alcoves with wide windows that would protect her privacy without giving up her security. Besides, she walked to the place each week to exchange her books for new ones and she often went alone. It was the one place where she did so.

But when? Not tomorrow—she could not face Cristo

Wellingham quite so soon. Wednesday was the morning she generally chose as her day to visit the reading rooms and if she stuck to routine she would be much safer.

With a quick scrawl she instructed him on the time and the place and, sealing the letter, put it in her reticule to post.

Chapter Six

Cristo sat by the window in a chair allowing him good access to the arrangement of the rooms. Eleanor Westbury was late by about twenty minutes, but he had decided to wait just in case some unforeseen difficulty had waylaid her.

He was glad that he had when he saw a figure dressed in deep blue hurrying in the door and, when she tipped her face to look around and her visage was seen beneath her ample summer hat, he knew it to be her.

Standing so that she might see the movement, he waited, though she did not come over immediately, but went to the desk instead and placed a pile of books before a small, efficient-looking man.

The librarian, Cristo guessed. He saw her speak to him for a few moments before traversing the room, picking one book from this shelf and another from the next. He doubted that she truly wished to read such tomes when he noticed one to be on the progress of the burgeoning railways, a book he had already struggled through a few months before.

Still, with an armful of reading material, she had given herself an excuse to wend her way towards the chairs at his end of the room, for there were places here to sit undisturbed and make one's choice as to what to take home.

'Lord Cristo! I do hope that we can make this very quick,' she said as she finally stood before him.

Her voice was exactly as he remembered it, though now she spoke in English, the King's English, each vowel rounded and proper, a thread of irritation easily heard.

'Thank you for coming, Lady Dromorne.'

Her whole face blushed bright as their eyes caught and he noticed that her hands shook as she sat down and placed the chosen books in her lap.

'I cannot stay very long at all, my lord.'

'Are you recovered from your *malade* of the other day?' Damn, he should not have used the French word for illness, he thought, for the frown on her forehead deepened considerably. He regrouped. 'You look very different…' Another mistake. He usually prided himself on his tact, and yet here he was like a tongue-tied and obtuse youth.

Fury marred the blueness of her eyes.

'Different?' she whispered, the anger in it making her undertone hoarse. 'If it is the past that you are referring to, I should think that it might be wise to know that I should not hesitate to relate back to your family your own part in our unfortunate meeting, should you choose to be indiscreet, my lord.'

He ignored her rebuke. 'Why were you there, then? In Paris, at the Château?' He wanted to add 'dressed as a whore', but the rawness of the word in the light of all she had become seemed inappropriate and so he tempered his query.

She looked around, checking the nearness of any listening ears. 'I was in the city visiting a good friend and I was at the Château Giraudon because of my own foolishness.'

'You came in with the other women there that evening? Women who were prostitutes.' He could no longer skirt around the issue.

She nodded. 'I had heard that the Parisian fashionable set were somewhat…daring in their dress, or their lack of it. I took it to be a truth when we were all bundled inside together. I certainly had no thought to join them.'

'God.'

'The brandy, however, was all my own fault and I have not touched a drop of alcohol since.'

'God,' he repeated again, and drew his hand through his hair. Not her fault, but his own. He should have seen that she was everything the others were not, should have read the clues with more acumen and aptitude. He was a man paid for uncovering duplicity, after all, and yet he had let himself be duped by a pretty face and an unexpected gift. His conscience pricked sharp. If a man had treated his sister as he had treated Eleanor, he would have killed him.

Cristo suddenly wished he could have spirited her away to some far-off and unreachable location, and one where he could replace the lines of worry on her forehead with laughter and ease.

He was surprised how very much he wanted that.

Yet still there were unanswered questions! 'There was a letter left in the folds of the bed-coverings that morning when you left. I presume it was your doing?'

'It was.'

'Had you read the missive?'

'The envelope was sealed in wax. I would hardly break my dead grandfather's trust.'

'Your grandfather?'

'I was Eleanor Bracewell-Lowen before marrying Martin Westbury, the Earl of Dromorne. Nigel was my brother.'

Her short, sharp nod encompassed a wealth of censure and the history between them solidified again. Every time he met this lady his world spun into an unbidden and opposite direction.

Nigel Bracewell-Lowen's blood dripping onto his hands as he tried to stem the flow from the wound in his throat, the empty brandy bottle before them denoting another evening of unbridled excess. Wild youth and wilder morals. Consequences had had no credence in the riotous foolhardy waywardness of Cristo's pubescence. Until Nigel!

'My father killed himself the following year.' Her voice again, layering guilt. 'So it is well that you know that you have already taken the full measure of happiness from my family.'

He shook his head, at a loss for words as he reached out for her hand, and in that second he knew that he had just made the second biggest mistake of his life.

It was like the newfangled electricity tingling up his arm and pouring into the very depths of his soul, filling it up with need, lust, urgency and spineless warmth.

Snatching his fingers away, he looked straight at her. The blood had run from her face, the blush now a pale and ghostly white as the books on her lap fell to the floor.

Everyone looked. The librarian with his thick spectacles,

the two women over by the door, and the group of men who perused the latest daily newssheets! Yet instead of bending to pick up the volumes, he could do nothing save gaze back at her and remember.

Remember the way she had felt beneath him, lying on burgundy velvet as he had teased her into response. Remember her wetness and abandon and seduction.

'Can I help you, sir?' The man at the desk was now right beside him. 'Are you quite well, Lady Dromorne?'

Cristo had to give Eleanor her due as she smiled and turned to the librarian, her voice husky.

'I am all right, thank you, Mr Jones. This gentleman was just asking me about the lending system here. He is new to London and it seems that he may want to join.'

The librarian's face brightened considerably.

'If you will follow me to the desk then, sir, I would be pleased to show you the details.'

Cristo stood, just as Eleanor did, her wedding ring catching the light when she straightened her bonnet. Further and further away from the woman in Paris, the fetters of responsibility and obligation chained across feeling. Married. Happily.

He could do nothing save stand and watch her leave, and the hand with which he had touched her lay fisted tight in the pocket of his jacket, fingers curled around self-reproach.

She should not have gone, should not have met him alone or allowed him to touch her, because now blackmail was the very least of her worries.

Leaning back against the seat beneath the trees in one

corner of Hyde Park, she liked the way summer crept into the shadows. Misty almost, overlaid with the dust of sunshine. Her heart beat with a rhythm she had felt only once before and she pressed down hard on the sensation, needing this small time to recover her wits.

Forgotten. Alive. Decadent. Intemperate.

Martin's age and impotence had been the one reason that she had accepted his proposal of marriage and the core of her contentment with him had been unquestioned until today.

Until Cristo Wellingham's fingers had unleashed a feeling in her body that was undeniable. Like water to a desert, unfolding into life, again, unbidden, and the crouching chaos ready to strike just as it had before.

Well, she could not let it!

Martin preferred the quiet life and the unexpected was not to be encouraged. 'A peaceful life is a happy life,' he was fond of saying, such a sentiment appealing after the débâcle in Paris. Her hands threaded themselves through the supple leather strap of her reticule, tying knots with her fingers. She did not catch the eye of a single person walking by, but sat very still, summoning calm.

'Lady Dromorne?' The question came quietly; looking up, Eleanor saw Lady Beatrice-Maude Wellingham had stopped before her.

Smoothing out the crinkles in her gown, Eleanor tucked back her hair before standing. She knew Beatrice-Maude Wellingham only slightly and when the woman dismissed her maid to a respectable distance worry blossomed.

'How fortunate to find you here, Lady Dromorne, for there

is a small matter that I wish to speak to you about that has been rather a worry to me.'

Eleanor indicated the seat next to her and the other sat as she did. 'I hope, then, that I might be of assistance.'

'It is a matter pertaining to my brother-in-law, Cristo Wellingham.'

The name lay between them like an unsheathed dagger, sharp and brutal, and Eleanor was lost for a reply.

'As you may be aware, he has returned home after many years abroad and as a family we would very much like him to stay in England. It is in that respect that I am seeking your counsel.'

'My counsel?' The words were choked out, almost inaudible, and Beatrice-Maude Wellingham looked at her strangely.

'Perhaps this is not a good time to worry you with anything,' she began. 'If your health is fragile after the theatre...'

'No, I am perfectly recovered.'

Eleanor hated the panic she could hear on the edge of denial and the question she could determine in the eyes of the one opposite.

'Very well. It is just that it has come to my notice that you may have a vested interest in seeing my brother-in-law unsettled here in England.'

'Your notice?' Everything she had feared was coming about. Had Cristo Wellingham confided the truth of her predicament to his family?

'Through various sources, you understand, and most of them quite reliable.' The woman opposite seemed to have no idea of the horror that was fast consuming Eleanor. 'I realize, of course, that the whole predicament may be rather difficult for you, but hoped that charity might persuade you to see the facts as we see them.'

'As you see them?'

'Many years have since passed and as his crime was only one of passion...'

Only one of passion!

Eleanor had had quite enough and she stood. 'I am not certain why you have brought this to my attention, Lady Beatrice-Maude, but I would prefer it if you would leave! The truth of my relations with your brother-in-law is something I do not wish to discuss and if he is adamant about ruining my reputation, then rest assured I shall fight him until the very last breath I take. I have my daughter to consider, after all, and any of his defamations of my character will be strongly denied in any forum you might name. I might add that the amount of my husband's money is endless and dragging any matter through the law courts would be prohibitively expensive.'

'His defamations?' Beatrice-Maude looked more than shocked. 'It was not his defamations I was referring to, Lady Dromorne, but your own. I know that he was involved in the scandal concerning the death of your brother and I thought to smooth the waters, so to speak, and find a resolution to such a loss.'

'My brother?' The world turned again 'You are speaking of Nigel?'

'Indeed. It was said at the time that Cristo was responsible for the accident.'

'I see.' Eleanor swallowed back bile. My God, she had, in her fear, read the whole situation completely wrongly, and given away things that she had admitted to no one else. Her fingers squeezed together. Beatrice-Maude Wellingham was one of the cleverest women in London. The cleverest, were rumour to be believed, and she had just laid the bare facts of the relationship right into her hands.

She hardly knew what to do next; did not trust herself with any other utterance, the horrible realisation of exposing everything a potent reason to keep her mouth firmly closed.

Finally Beatrice-Maude spoke. 'I think I should probably take my leave.'

'I think that you probably should.' Eleanor could no longer cope with pretending manners. Sparring with two Wellinghams in one day was more than enough.

She watched as the older woman turned, though she did not walk away immediately.

'You may count on my saying nothing of this matter to anyone, Lady Dromorne.' Her words were softly said, as if she was cognisant of the importance of care.

'A service that I would thank you for, Lady Beatrice-Maude.' Eleanor did not stand, but waited till the footsteps receded before looking up. The wind was heightening, buffeting itself against the leaves and sending a few of them scattering in the air.

She held herself tight with silence, the mute reserve helping her to come to terms with the gravity of her mistake.

Stupid. Stupid. Stupid.

Could she trust the woman? Would Beatrice-Maude

Wellingham be true to her word of maintaining her silence? The thicker tie of blood would make things more difficult and, looking at the family group the other evening, she had detected a strong sense of solidarity. Too strong?

When Martin called her as she arrived home some half an hour later, she pinched colour into her cheeks before walking out to greet him, for none of this could ever be his problem and his health was fragile. Slipping her hand into his, she kissed him on the cheek, leaning against the handles of his chair for balance.

'When will Florencia be home?' he asked her. 'Her governess said that she was not here yet.'

'Soon, I think. Your sister has taken her out for the afternoon.'

'You look pale.'

'I sat in the park on the way home from the reading room and it was a little chilly. Lady Beatrice-Maude Wellingham stopped to ask how we were.'

How easy it was to stretch out the truth when all your life depended on it, Eleanor thought.

His hand squeezed her own. 'Sometimes I worry that I have made your life very dull, my dear.'

She stopped him simply by raising her hand to his face. The stubble of an eight-hour shadow scratched and she noticed the way his skin had shrunk around the bones of his cheek.

Thinner. Older. More tired.

His fingers interlaced with hers. A good and honourable man, and a long way from the husband that she would have struggled to find had the true enormity of her predicament ever become public. No, she was the most fortunate of women and if the sacrifice of marital intimacy was the payment for respectability, then far be it from her to wish it different.

As he continued to stroke the back of her hand, however, worrying her skin with a dull repetition, she wondered how it was possible for Cristo Wellingham's simple touch to engender a reaction that had raced through all her body.

'I would like to hold a party, Taris, to celebrate Cristo's return.' Beatrice entwined her feet through those of her husband's as they lay in bed later that night. His warmth was welcomed.

She felt his chest rise in laughter, the darkness of the room obscuring any expression. 'I am not certain he would welcome such a thing. I know I should not. Besides, as yet we have no real idea of his motives for returning to England. He may be here to slander the name of Wellingham yet again and will leave as soon as he gets bored by the uneventful routine of everyday life.'

'He is your brother, Taris. Whatever happens, you will need to mend your fences or face a lifetime of regret.'

'Asher would rather erect higher barriers and push him out altogether. The sins in his past have not been simple and when he left last time the arguments between our father and Cristo were, at the least, vitriolic. He was a wild youth, I suppose, with few boundaries, though Ashborne always kept a certain distance from him, which probably made matters worse.'

Beatrice broke in with her own understanding of the matter. 'Yet he is not an evil man, or even a bad one.'

His smile curved into the tips of her fingers. 'You can tell so quickly?'

'I was married to a miscreant for years. One gets a feel for them.'

'Lord, Bea. Sometimes your wit is careless...'

Her laughter drifted across the room. 'Only with you, Taris,' she said softly, her nails running across the bare skin of his arm, before she returned to the matter in hand. 'It could be a weekend house party down at Beaconsmeade. Not a huge affair, but a small one.'

'Who would you invite?'

Bea felt her heart begin to race a little faster, for deception was something she had always been very bad at. 'The family, of course, and a few other friends and acquaintances.'

His palm took her wrist, measuring the beat. 'Acquaintances?' There was a tone in the word demanding truth.

'I saw Lady Dromorne today in the park, Taris. Did your brother ever mention her to you?'

Taris pushed back his pillow. 'Eleanor Westbury? In what way?'

'Had he been...interested in her at all?'

'Did she say that he had been?'

'No.' Even to her own ears the denial was too quick. Too forced.

'There was that fracas many years ago with Nigel Bracewell-Lowen that many insisted was a result of Cristo's antics, though of course such an accusation was never proved. I do not think that she would welcome your invitation. Besides, she is a married woman and Martin Westbury rarely ventures out.'

Bea nodded. Reason pointed to a happy union, but her own intuition was telling her something very different. Lady Dromorne had fainted when she had seen Cristo at the theatre and this afternoon Prudence Tomlinson had mentioned she had seen them touching hands in the public reading room.

Bea had squashed this rumour by swearing her brother-in-law to be at Beaconsmeade for the day and Prue had laughed at her own silly imagination, glad for the chance to clear up such a misunderstanding. Yet the meeting with Eleanor had made Bea curious.

How could Cristo's revelations be responsible for ruining Eleanor's reputation? Her mind ran further afield to the age and infirmity of the husband. There was a daughter, too, of about five, if memory served her well. She wondered how such an unwell and aged man had been able to father a child. Another thought charged in over the top of that one and Beatrice took in a breath. What if Martin Westbury was not the true parent of Eleanor's daughter? Cursing her fertile imagination, she listened again to her husband.

'If you are bent on repairing the relations between our family, perhaps an invitation to the two younger Westbury nieces might be a better way to do it. They are reputed to be sensible girls. Ask some of the young bucks about Beaconsmeade to even out the numbers.'

Beatrice smiled tightly. Sense told her to leave the matter entirely, yet there was sadness in the pale blue eyes of Eleanor Westbury that was undeniably interlaced with her brother-in-law. The small opportunity to play out the conclusion of something important could not hurt, could it?

She snuggled down into the arms of her husband and pulled the light cover across them, his heavy masculinity treasured and safe.

'I love you, Taris.'

He laughed as he turned her over, and covered the soft desire in her body with his own particular molten heat.

'Show me.'

Chapter Seven

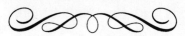

The invitation to the Wellinghams' party in ten days' time caused a stir in the Dromorne household and for many more reasons than any could have guessed.

The two younger Westbury girls screamed with delighted shock, each imagining the gowns that might catch the fancy and admiration of the enigmatic youngest Wellingham brother.

Martin Westbury, on the other hand, decided that he would simply decline the invite altogether, but was most insistent that his wife take his nieces and sister to the affair as it had been a long while since they had been invited to any soirée of the very first order. Not that Martin ranked things in accordance with such strict and rigid axioms, but his sister's daughters' futures had to be considered and another Season in London for the girls was beginning to pall on him with the hustle and bustle social intercourse demanded.

Eleanor was just struck dumb, unable to formulate any real understanding of any of it.

She had expected to be a *persona non grata* to Lady

Beatrice-Maude after her outburst and instead had received one of the most sought-after social cards of the Season. A great dread engulfed her.

'Sophie and Margaret must go, of course,' she began, and was surprised when Martin raised his hand.

'You and Diana will chaperone them, Lainie. It is only right and proper.'

'I am quite happy to let Diana go in my stead. Besides, I could not leave Florencia for so very long.'

But her husband was having none of it.

'As Florencia has her beloved governess and I have been feeling considerably better of late, I am certain this would be a good change for all of us.' He winked at his sister. 'To make sure that we live up to the standards required, you shall all go off to the dressmaker and get fitted out for such an occasion.'

Such a proclamation brought renewed shouts of delight, Margaret's face even teasing a smile from the gloom that had overcome Eleanor, and when Florencia was brought down, Eleanor opened her arms to her daughter, enjoying her soft warmth.

'Did you have a lovely time yesterday, Florencia?' Margaret asked the question with a smile.

'We saw some puppies. They licked my hands and followed me. Could we bring one home, Mama, even just for a little while?' The silver in her hair was caught by the light from the window.

'You know that Papa would get iller if a pet came home, darling.'

'We could keep one outside, though? Aunt Diana's friend said that it could be.'

'It might get rather cold in the winter when you are warmly tucked up in your bed.'

Eleanor wished Martin would help her out on this, but his earlier forcefulness was gone, replaced instead by the more normal air of exhaustion. Even the scrambled eggs seemed too much bother for him to eat this morning. A pang of worry shot through her, her own concerns seeming selfish in the face of his sickness.

'Should I ask the doctor to come and see you again, Martin? He is most happy to be called at any time.'

Her husband shook his head and closed his eyes, momentarily looking so washed out that a flurry of alarm made Eleanor start. When Florencia glanced up from her lap, she ordered herself to be calm. The doctor had assured them that his condition was stable and that the deterioration Eleanor could so plainly see had tapered off. She wanted to seek a second opinion, but Martin would have none of it, insisting on his satisfaction with such a prognosis.

Hugging Florencia tighter, she wondered if his condition would continue to worsen. In the breakfast room, with the happy talk of new gowns and the sun slanting through the French doors from the outside courtyard, such a thought was unsettling; an interloping truth that she wanted to ignore until she no longer could. The scent of summer roses in a large blue vase filled the air.

Taking a breath, she gathered her strength and joined in the conversation Margaret and Sophie were having on the dressmaker of their choice and on the weekend's entertainment.

'They say that Beaconsmeade is a beautiful old house and that Lord Taris Wellingham keeps his best horses at stud there.' Sophie seemed full of information that Eleanor had not a notion of.

'Perhaps there will be a chance to ride, then, for Cristo Wellingham is reported to be keen on the sport. I will put in my riding habit.'

Margaret's hopes had Sophie giggling, though the youthful exuberance of the girls gave Eleanor a sharp pang of loss.

When had she ever been truly young? Pregnant at eighteen and a wife before twenty! And now with her twenty-fourth birthday on the horizon she felt old before her time. Stolen kisses would never be for her, the flirtatious dance of the fan in a crowded ballroom only a figment of imagination and fantasy, like some chapter of one of the romantic books she sometimes borrowed from the reading room.

Beaconsmeade suddenly felt like a trap! A terrible mistake that she was being drawn into. If Cristo Wellingham should be caught in the wiles of her beautiful nieces, what would happen then?

A lifetime of trying not to touch him or be alone with him or letting the truth of her lost year become public knowledge, for with a single misplaced glance her whole life could fall to pieces. So very, very easily.

Looking up, she saw Martin watching her in that peculiar way he had of seeing straight through a person.

'Penny for your thoughts.' She smiled, but he did not

answer, the melancholy that was growing in him with each passing week so much more apparent amongst a roomful of sunshine, roses and hopeful expectations.

The evening fell across the land as Cristo rode down towards the shore, faster than safety might allow him, the breath of his horse caught in mist, white-shadowed warmth amidst all that was cold.

Home at Falder! Finally. He had come alone and late, the knowledge of an empty castle making it easier to journey here. He intended to return to London in the morning, after looking at the Graveson land.

Yet the ocean breathed its welcome, the foam of a fading storm caught in the pebbles and on the wind, tumbling into distance and lost. He laughed at the fragility of all that the sea could throw at him, her tendrils lapping at the feet of his mount as on and on he galloped, the bold speed of Demeter eating up the miles. Falder Castle lay far behind, the numerous turrets caught by the last pink rays of dusk, the new quarter moon hiding behind clouds of high cirrus tinged with red.

The anger in him settled into something more akin to acceptance and the wide-open freedom soothed a fury that had gripped him ever since he had touched Eleanor Westbury's hand.

She was not for him!

Never for him!

The refrain beat across denial and desire and just plain damned common sense.

He had come home to become the person that he once

had been, a son, a brother, a lord. He had not ventured into England to become a home-wrecker or a heartbreaker or a rake. The memory of Paris must be left there, forgotten, buried amongst the necessity of survival and civility. For too many years he had let the other side rule him; whether for the good of mankind or for the good of himself, he had got to the point where he could no longer tell, his forays into the underbelly of greed and falsity the only thing that let him believe anything mattered. Spying for the British had almost cost him his sanity, the company he had kept for years far away from any fellowship he might have enjoyed otherwise. Yet he saw the sacrifice as a penance and the recklessness in him had been tethered instead into the benefit of England's protection and sovereignty. He was pleased that it had ended, that the Foreign Office had released him from further duties when his file had been closed.

Breathing out hard, he stopped and the light on the calmer waters of the peninsula of Return Home Bay was a perfect reflection of the sky. As unreal as he was, only mirroring what was outside, what was expected, the heavy burden of his name and his heritage finally grounding the fury of all that had happened in his life.

He remembered Nigel's life-blood ebbing away and his own blood on the deck of the nightmare ship he had taken from London, fleeing from his father's wrath and banishment! The blood of other souls in Paris was mixed in there, too, politics and persuasion exacting their own biting revenge. Sometimes he had killed innocents and then reasoned the sin gone by patriotic virtue. Sometimes at night he remembered those faces, the last expressions of terror etched for ever into his own regret. He frowned. The retribution of ghosts was surprisingly relentless and his own contrition undeniably growing.

Dismounting, he stooped to pick up a pebble, skipping it across the surface in the way that he had learnt in his youth. Lord, what mistakes he had made!

Time folded back and he was on the front steps of Nigel's parents' home, the story of a son's demise full on his lips. On his lips until the door had been opened and the man who had stood there was the same one who had shot at them unexpectedly from the bridge behind the village cemetery. The recognition had been as fatal as Cristo's lack of gumption, and though he had thought to run by then it was far, far too late. Nigel's uncle had told him that he had seen the boys using guns for target practice; when Cristo had argued the point the man had become angry, blaming the alcohol the boys had drunk for skewing his memory. An accident was a thing of chance, after all, the older man had added, and no one needed to be ruined by it.

Cristo had returned to London that very night to tell his father the true version of events, but Ashborne had refused to believe his side of the story and had banished him to France on the next tide, forbidding him to return to England for a very long time. Faced with his father's rejection, Nigel's uncle's slanderous untruths and a reputation that was hardly salubrious, he had boarded the ship, nearly nineteen but with the cares of the world firmly embedded on his shoulders.

Cristo swore as he remembered Eleanor's words.

'Know that you have already taken the full measure of happiness from my family.'

Another sin. A further damnation!

Falder spoke to him with the wisdom of generations enfolded in its soil, a prudent and enlightened message that bore the weight of ancestry reaching back into living history, and beyond, his body only a vassal of wardship for the few paltry years that God had allotted to him.

Eight-and-twenty gone, many frittered away in the quest for a justice that he himself had never gained. A wanderer. A stranger. A lover. A spy. A man with as many faces as he had needed: the list as endless as the sea, and as changing. But for now he wanted permanence. Bending down again, he filtered a handful of sand through his fingers and watched it fall onto a shore that was known, understood and cherished.

Tears blurred his eyes and he wiped them away with the cloth of his jacket, quickly, shaken by the depth of his love for the place and he knelt on the living and breathing ground, praying aloud to the Lord for deliverance.

'Forgive me, Father, for I have sinned...'

Eleanor saw Lord Cristo in the park a few days later, his head a good couple of inches above those of the men about him and the material of his jacket straining across the breadth of his back. She was glad he was looking away, for it gave her a chance to seek out another trail that would lead her nowhere near him. The sun in his hair marked it with every shade of pale, the length creeping onto the material of his collar and tousled thick. She turned her gold wedding ring and remembered the feel of him beneath her fingers before hot guilt made her heart beat faster.

Angling the broad brim on her bonnet, she tipped her head, slicing off the whole end of the pathway.

She had slept badly in the past few days, dreams and nightmares entwined with shame and forbidden passion and banishing her to church early each dawn to pray for some ease from the sins of the flesh. The image of Jesus stretched on the cross in the stained glass etching was a timely reminder of what might happen to her should her indiscretion ever be known. She smiled at the word 'indiscretion' for it intimated such a small mistake, an ill-chosen pathway of moderate consequence. The truth of her ruin and loss was something far more brutal.

Two shiny brown boots suddenly blocked her path and she knew exactly to whom they belonged even before she looked up.

'Ma'am.' Cristo Wellingham gave her his greeting, eyes in the sunshine much lighter than she had seen them.

Beautiful eyes, her daughter's eyes!

The very thought chased away fright and replaced it with a channelled resolve. Quietly asking her maid to allow her some space to talk, she walked over to the shelter of a line of elms and stopped there.

No one was in sight save her servant, and farther off two old men whom she did not know. Five moments at the most, she thought, and took a breath.

'Your sister-in-law sent an invitation for a soirée at Beaconsmeade. Did you know that she had done so?'

He shook his head.

'You of all people must realise that I cannot possibly

come.' She kept her voice as low as she might manage it and the frown on his brow indicated thought.

'Because it might compromise your carefully constructed public persona?' He stepped back as her glance raked across his, anger and uncertainty and sheer desperation melded with another growing truth. 'Are you happily married, Lady Dromorne?'

The veneer of civilisation that he had affected here in England was suddenly much less obvious. Eleanor tasted fear as she never had before, because in the bare, cold amber she detected something she had seen in her own eyes in the mirror over the past few days.

Longing.

Longing that even anger and vigilance and sense had failed to dislodge. She stood wordless, the dreadful chasm of loss between them echoing in every breath that she took.

Tell him, yes, I am very happily married, she heard her mind say. *Tell him that you love your husband and your life and your place in the world and that any interference from him would be most unwelcome and unacceptable. Tell him to go and to never look back and insist that the history between them was so repugnant she needed no more reminding of any of it.*

She opened her mouth and then closed it again, the warm summer wind streaming between them and the silk of her dress touching her skin in the way he had once touched it, inviting passion, igniting lust.

Even for Florencia she could not say the words.

'Meet me tonight. I have rooms here in London…' He spoke as she did not.

Pulled from the past into the present, this harsh truth of seduction was a far easier thing to counter.

She could not believe he had said such words to her here in the wind and in the sunlight. A man who would throw away her good name on a whim, never even imagining whom else he would hurt. 'My husband loves me, Lord Cristo, and I am a wife who applauds loyalty.'

'Touch me, then.'

Shock filled her eyes.

'Touch me and tell me that there is nothing at all left between us.'

She held her fists tight against her skirt. 'The pull of flesh is only a fleeting thing, *monseigneur*.' The title she gave him was deliberate, a grim reminder of the misunderstanding that trembled beneath anger. 'Honour and trust and duty are the tenets that a sensible woman lives by.'

'And you are sensible?'

'Very.' The word was as forceful as she could make it, moulded by her depth of fear.

Unexpectedly, he took three steps back. 'Logic and reason run a poor second to the heat of passion, *ma chérie*. Should you relax your guard for a moment, the truth of all you deny might be a revelation to you.'

Pursing her lips, Eleanor allowed him no leeway. 'I do not think you should presume to believe that you know anything of my fidelity. My life has changed completely since Paris and I am a woman who learns well from her mistakes.'

'Mistakes?' He echoed the word, turning it on his tongue as if trying to understand the very nature of its meaning before finding a retort. 'I have relegated our night together to neither blunder nor error. Indeed, were I to give it a label, as you seem want to do, I might have chanced something very different.'

The glint in his eye was so carnal and lascivious that Eleanor knew exactly where he would have placed it. The smile he gave her showed off his gleaming white teeth.

Biting back impatience, she inclined her head as he gave her his leave without another word, his figure receding into the distance until he was lost altogether when the next corner claimed him.

It was over between them, the truth of circumstance bitingly clear: just a matter of the flesh, easily duplicated in a room for rent by the hour.

Turning, she watched the ducks on the lake in their small family groups. Mother. Father. Ducklings. How it should be. How it had been designed and planned. Florencia knew who her parents were and without Martin, Eleanor might never have made it back to England. Dark days and lonely days. Days when she had wondered if it might not have been easier to simply cease to exist at all. Pressing down on her chest in alarm, she tried to breathe, her composure reasserting itself as the tableau before her took shape. The trees, the birds, the pathways, people now further afield and the distant clatter of hooves.

A good life. Untainted and wholesome. A real life.

Her life.

Not thrilling or adventurous or even passionate, but safe and prudent and certain.

With a wave of her hand she gestured her maid forwards, resolutely ignoring the question in her eyes as she struck down the pathway for home, hating the tears that blurred everything before her. Disappointment lent her gait a tense anger that was almost as unreal as her honour, dissolved under the meaning of Cristo Wellingham's words.

Meet me tonight. I have rooms here in London.

Only that. Only that.

The words rolled around in the empty corridors of her hope, a bitter pill pointing to the real character of a man of whom she had no true knowledge. It was done between them. Finished. Her nails dug into her palms, causing hurt until she released her grip and opened her fingers to the air.

Chapter Eight

The dinner at the Baxters' was unavoidable, as an invitation had been sent and accepted weeks in advance.

It was the first time she had been out in society since the fiasco at the Haymarket Theatre and Eleanor was pleased that the gathering was a small one.

Cristo Wellingham would not be there.

He frequented the more racy events by all the news she was given through her nieces' fascination with the man. The age of all those present tonight promised to be well over fifty and the host was a devout man who countenanced no form of rudeness or vulgarity. The very thought made her swallow, for if Anthony Baxter had an inkling of her past she would not get a foot in the doorway.

Anger welled. The headstrong exuberance of her youth was hardly a fault that should lead to such consequences and had she not made up for her mistakes ever since with a pious and selfless existence? Hiding everything.

She jolted as Martin came into the room, for she had not heard the whirr of the wheels on the chair.

'You are so jumpy these days, Eleanor, and in one so young it is rather worrying. You need to get out more, for Florencia is well able to cope without your presence in the house for a few hours.'

In the light of her thoughts from a few moments prior, the criticism stung more than it might have otherwise. 'I am quite happy as I am,' she returned, hearing in her retort an anger that was not becoming, but today, with her carefully constructed world in danger of falling apart, any censure rankled.

'If I could venture on a word, "distracted" might be the one to describe you of late, and it doesn't suit you.' He held his cravat out to her and she took it. 'Would you help me with this?'

She had always tied his cravat, though today she felt irritation as she finished off the last of the intricate folds. She was distracted. Distracted to the point of bewilderment. She pushed down on the feeling as he lifted a box she had not noticed from his lap and gave it to her.

Garrard's, the jewellers? When she opened the case a necklace of turquoise lay in the velvet with matching earrings beside it.

'It is not my birthday for another month…?' she began, questioningly.

'No. But you have seemed preoccupied and I thought a tonic in order. Besides it is almost five years ago that I asked you to marry me and I wanted to remember that.'

Eleanor's mind went back: Florence in the summer with its plane trees sculptured green and the Arno winding its way in front of the villa he owned beside the Piazza della

Signoria. They had been sitting in the gazebo when she had felt nauseous and he had brought her out a warm wet towel scented in lavender to wipe her face and hands.

Luxury after the débâcle in France. A man who might take care of everything, even a daughter conceived out of wedlock on a gaudy velvet bed in the Chateau Giraudon.

Stroking one turquoise stone and then another, the sheer goodness of her husband left her speechless. 'I have never deserved you, Martin.'

He stopped her words by a touch against her arm, no passion in it. 'If I had been younger, healthier...'

With a shake of her head she leant down and gave him a kiss on the cheek, wishing just for a moment that she might have wanted passion and found his lips. But she did not wish to spoil everything with a careless gesture and five years of togetherness had never included any sort of lust.

'Would you wear these today?' he asked and she bent as he fastened the stones, the gold adjusting quickly to the temperature of her skin.

When he had finished she walked to the mirror and saw a woman of means looking back, the necklace lavish and expensive, the bodice of the gown adorned in Honiton lace and her hair fashioned in a style that might suit...an older woman.

The thought came from nowhere. A woman who was cautious, and careful and proper! Forcing gaiety as she turned back to her husband, she thanked him for her gift.

Cristo noticed Eleanor Westbury the moment she walked into the small salon, her husband in the chair before her.

This evening she wore a gown of much the same cut as the older female guests, the bodice high and proper and a heavy turquoise bauble of gold and blue sitting in the lace. Did the Earl of Dromorne choose her clothes as well as her jewellery? He wondered how wealth seemed bent on squandering taste with such dreadful choices.

Close up the man was more ancient than he had imagined him at the theatre, though the grey in his hair was not as pronounced as he had first thought it.

Sixty, he imagined. Or nearly sixty. The image of Eleanor lying in bed with her husband brought a vision he did not wish for and he dismissed it, the lingering memory of their own tryst replacing the illusion.

Satin skin and warmth, the sounds of winter Paris and its Sunday bells, soft mist across the Seine coating the charcoal branches of elms in greyness. She had a presence he had never quite fathomed. Haunting. Calling. A woman who had stirred his blood in a way no other had ever managed to do before or since.

Did Martin Westbury now feel the same pleasure? He noticed how the man placed his fingers across her arm in a singular proclamation of ownership, and noticed too the way her fingers curled about his in return. Anger blossomed, though given his own part in the débâcle in Paris it was guilt that should have surfaced. He was the one, after all, who had left a young lady ruined in a strange and foreign city, a man who should have behaved differently and more honourably. If he could take it back he would. If he could have the moment again he would have kept her safe and unscathed, a tiny incident that would cause only a ripple in the fabric of Eleanor Dromorne's life.

And instead? He did not like to even think of what had happened after she had disembarked from the carriage that he had sent her away in!

With a sigh he looked up and straight into the eyes of Honour Baxter, the wife of his host.

'She is beautiful, no?' Her accent was marked, the French slurring the words into a longer version of the English.

Cristo realised that she spoke of Lady Dromorne and schooled all expression on his face.

'Indeed.'

'But sad I think, too. A young flower who has not yet had the chance to open.'

He remained silent.

'I knew her mother, you know. A melancholic woman who was constantly worried about her health. Eleanor was always different, for she was vibrant and alive in a way few other girls her age were. I often wonder just what happened to douse such…passion?'

Her legs entwined about his own. Her teeth nipping at his throat.

Hardly passionless!

What happened after she had left him and disappeared into a waking day?

Where had she met Dromorne and why had she married a man old enough to be her father?

Necessity! The answer came unbidden and rang with the clearness of an unwanted truth.

Had she rolled the dice and taken her chances? An older

man who might not notice a lack of maidenhead and a lie that would suck the living out of anybody. And had.

Passionless.

Now?

Because of him?

The awful verity of such a thought almost brought him to his knees and the first stab of pain in his head made him worry.

Lord help her, Eleanor thought, Cristo Wellingham was here, in this room not five yards away and speaking with the host's wife, Honour Baxter, a Frenchwoman who had made her home in London for many years.

Her fingers tightened across those of her husband and as he patted her hand she held on, the turquoise stones in her new necklace glinting under a fine chandelier above them, pinning her into the light, like an insect under glass. When Cristo Wellingham's eyes suddenly found hers she looked away and for the first time in a long while she swore beneath her breath, sheer fury reshaping her more normal careful-ness. The skin on her arms rose up into goose-bumps as he came closer and she steeled herself to greet him.

'Lord Cristo. I don't believe you have met the Earl of Dromorne and his charming young wife, Lady Dromorne.' Anthony Baxter gave the introductions as Martin held out his hand. Eleanor merely nodded, her title and sex affording her the ability to remain as glacial as she wished.

'My wife was delighted with Lord Cristo's return from Paris as she now has someone to reminisce on the beauty of a city that has long been in her heart. Have you spent much time there, Lady Dromorne?'

Eleanor shook her head. 'No, I am afraid not.'

'Then you must entice your husband there, my dear. It is in the spring when the city is at its most beautiful, would you not agree, my lord?'

'I would beg to differ and say that it is the season of winter that appeals to me the most, sir.'

Dark eyes bored straight into her own and the room tilted and then straightened, a bend in time that had her leaning against Martin's chair, the faint echo of bells in her mind and a man who wore too many rings upon his fingers. Embellished. Foreign. The weight of years of adventure scrawled into both his clothes and the furnishings of his room!

Surreptitiously she glanced at his hands to see them bare. Just another difference. Stripped of gold and silver in London, but with the same sense of recklessness still upon him, simmering in his height and his stance and in the rough beauty of his face.

'Did you live in Paris for long?' Martin's question was quietly phrased, his lisp giving the city's name a burnished edge.

'Too long.' Cristo Wellingham's reply held no hint of any such temperance and Eleanor wondered if her husband might have sensed his irony, but it seemed that he had not for his next question was even more to the point.

'I enjoyed the area around the Louvre the most when I was there last. Where did you reside?'

'Near Montmartre.'

Anthony Baxter coughed, the mention of a name that boasted more than its fair share of the evils of the night heard in the noise. An English gentleman's way of shelving a topic for a more pleasant one. She wondered at the smile that was momentarily on Lord Cristo's lips before he had the chance to hide it.

Neither tame nor amenable, he was a man who ruled a room with a sheer and easy power. The ache in her stomach leapt into fear and she was pleased when Honour Baxter took her by the arm and led her away to admire a recently completed tapestry.

Mon Dieu, Cristo thought, as the sixth course of the unending dinner was served, the formal English fare of lamb cutlets, chicken patties and lobster rissoles richer than he remembered, and heavy.

He wished he might have been seated somewhere near Eleanor Westbury but he was not, his place almost as far from hers as could be managed and the table splintering into groups that denied him even the pleasure of hearing her opinions.

Baxter was a man who took his position as a lay preacher with a depressing seriousness and every word he uttered seemed more and more conservative, the teachings of the Bible translated so literally Cristo could barely bother to listen. He had only deigned to come in the first place because of Honour, a woman whom he admired, with her quick laughter and relaxed ways. He wondered how her marriage had lasted the distance of time and reasoned perhaps opposites did in some way attract.

Still, the wine was a fine one, though a headache that was familiar had begun to pound, and he switched over to water to try to keep it at bay, alarmed by the tremors he felt in his hand as he lifted the glass to his lips. Beneath the thick layers of English cloth his body prickled with sweat; finishing the water, he poured himself another from the silver jug on the table in front of him and the liquid settled his stomach.

When the men finally joined the women later in the drawing room he noticed Eleanor alone at the window on the far side of the room. He was very careful not to touch her as he came close.

'I would like to apologise for my words the other day. They were ill put and you were right to chastise me for them.'

She said nothing, though the flints of ice in her eyes drew back into only blueness. Her hair curled in ringlets around the line of her face.

'You are easily the most beautiful woman in all of London town, though I suppose many have told you such.'

The line marking the skin between her eyes deepened. 'Perhaps, my lord, you have consumed too much of the wine the Baxter table is famous for.'

'You think my judgement so askew?'

Her bottom lip trembled, the fullness of it inviting notice. 'Askew and imprudent.' The words were said without any form of artifice and her fingers worried the oversized turquoise stones at her neck.

'Your husband must have surely—' She did not let him finish.

'My husband has many other more important things to occupy his time and besides, he knows that I do not demand such empty flattery.'

'If it were empty, I should never voice it.' He reached out for the sill to steady a sudden light-headedness, for the slur in his words was obvious. Lord, this attack was worse than all the others before it in the intensity and speed of its onslaught.

The pain in his temple blurred his vision, the room falling into a haze of yellow, and making him feel clammy and strange. Still, he had other things to ask her and for the moment they remained alone.

'My sister-in-law said she had seen you in the park the other day?' He was pleased his voice seemed more or less normal.

'Lady Beatrice-Maude?'

'Indeed.'

'I had hoped for her confidence.'

'Pardon?' The topic had got away with him somewhat and he could not discern the connection.

'Lady Beatrice-Maude? Is it on her bidding that you now approach me? Please do disregard anything that she might have inferred from our meeting, for I was not myself that day.'

He shook his head and tried to get the conversation to make sense. 'My brother's wife is usually very circumspect.'

'I made a mistake once and will never do so again.' Her hand touched his then, almost as a plea, and the world about them simply stopped. He felt as if they could have been anywhere, alone, singled out, adrift from all that held them tethered, floating into a place that was only theirs, his life-line in a stormy and wind-tossed sea.

'Eleanor.' He said her name as a lover might, the sweet music of it making him want to repeat it again and again as his fingers tightened about hers. For a moment she allowed such a caress, watching him, the knowledge of their small embrace mirrored in her pale blue gaze, softening with an unexpected yearning before being snatched away. The rounded shape of her derrière was all that was left to him as she rejoined her husband.

'Damn.' As he shook his head against the growing ache in his temple, the rush of pain made his brow wet and his hands relaxed as swirling lights of dizzy unbalance reached out to claim him.

Cristo Wellingham was deathly white, the pale set of his more usually bronzed skin visible even from a distance. He was trying to sit up, trying to make sense of what had happened and reclaim a lost control.

'The doctor should be here within a few moments.' Anthony Baxter's statement contained more than a measure of worry.

'No need.' Shakily moving his head from side to side, Cristo Wellingham dislodged the wet cloth draping his fore-head as shards of amber caught her glance again, drawing her in like finely-honed magnets, and the guilt and uncertainty that had blossomed in such a startling way when she had touched him a few moments ago returned.

The blond of his hair was darkened with sweat, the length of it resting upon his opened shirt, the skin of his chest easily seen in the parted fabric.

'I am…sorry.' He spoke to the room in general as he sat up, one hand on the sill of the window behind and the other on the arm of a sofa next to him. Eleanor knew instantly the effort it was costing him. 'I suffer from migraines and they recur from time to time. The English weather seems to bring them on.'

His voice held a note of steel and ice, though the smile that played across his face was there as a foil. A mask, showing only what might be shown at a party, his considerable illness consigned to mere nuisance.

'Does an episode last long?' Honour Baxter's question was brittle.

'No.' He was upright now, the ties of his cravat hanging in long folds against the dark of his jacket. A man who was seldom used to showing weakness in front of anyone, she guessed, and who was trying in the aftermath of exposure to minimise any appearance of blemish. He no longer looked her way as he made a show of thanking his host for the evening whilst apologising for his part in the spoiling of it.

When Anthony Baxter shook his head in the age-old tradition of a host denying even the hint of difficulty he took his leave, the energy and vitality in the room lessening with his departure and leaving only a dull and awkward silence.

Eleanor swallowed back all her tumbling thoughts even as her husband began to discuss the turn of events with the two men next to him.

Cristo Wellingham's migraine looked more debilitating than she had ever imagined one to be. Why was he not ensconced at Falder with his family if his health was so fragile?

His solitariness rankled and the wooden handles on her husband's chair were hard beneath her palms and so different from the living spark of skin she had felt as she had touched his arm. She hated the prick of tears behind her eyes and the empty ache in the back of her throat as she remembered the way his fingers had curled about her own.

'You did not tell us that you suffered so badly from headaches. The drawing rooms of this city were alight last evening with the news of your swoon yesterday at the Baxters'.' Ashe paced Cristo's bedroom with a decided purpose. His brother had arrived well before noon, to find him naked in bed, curled on his side, the covers pushed down, to allow the cool air to play across his sweat-covered shoulders. When Cristo turned over, Ashe did not look at all happy.

'I have had them for a long time...'

'Or that your back was riddled with scars. Where did you get them?'

'The boat I took when I left England made a small detour to the south of Spain. It was not a passenger ship, you understand, but a vessel intent on the pillaging of other more innocent sea-farers. I was young and fit and foolish enough to see some celestial justice inherent in robbing from the wealthy to give to the poor.'

'So you did not think to jump ship?'

'I did as soon as I was able, catching a ride from Barcelona to Paris. Ashborne had made it clear that my behaviour was abhorrent to him and I did not think he would have wished for any further plea for help.'

'And what of Taris and me? We heard nothing from you for years when you were in Paris except for a few terse notes demanding we stay out of your life.'

'I had imagined you felt the same way as our father did.'

'But the letters we sent…?'

'Went unopened. I saw no reason to revisit bad memories.'

'God, Cristo! You are twice as stubborn as Taris and that is saying something. I want you to come to Falder to recuperate.'

Cristo shook his head, the pillows behind him protesting the movement.

'You're ill, damn it! You need someone to look after you.'

'Milne has done it before.'

'Someone qualified.'

'Experience qualifies him.'

'And any lasting damage? Is that something we might be worried about?'

'If it was, I am certain such an affliction would have shown itself by now.' Reaching for his gold watch on the bedside table, he checked the time. The disturbances in his vision were much lessened this morning.

'If you would rather I left England altogether…?'

'And go where?'

'Europe. America. The East. The world is a big place

when nothing ties you down.' His easy drawl was so practised he almost believed his own indifference.

'Just roll in and roll out, you mean, after ten years of no
contact? I almost believe that you might do it. Well, brother,
you have not bargained on the whims of my wife and I tell
you now if I don't bring you home after this Emerald will
send Azziz and Toro to get you.'

'Who?'

'Men from the port of Kingston with rings in their ears
and swords in their hands.' Asher began to smile at his
explanation.

'As I remember it, you used to be less happy.'

Again he smiled.

'I keep hearing rumours that your wife was a pirate.'

'And you believe them?'

'Her minions fit the description.'

'Then it must be true.'

Cristo saw how he turned the golden ring on the third
finger of his left hand with infinite care.

'When I left you had just married Melanie.'

'When you left you still had ten fingers on your hands
and a hide on your back that was untarnished.'

'Things change.'

'And change again.'

'Meaning?'

'Second chances, Cristy.'

His old name. His nickname. He shook his head before
he knew that he had and watched Ashe cross to the bed and
sit down.

'Falder offers redemption to wearied souls and from what

I can see your soul is indeed wearied. Come home and heal.'

Cristo swallowed. Home in the company of his family? The secrets he needed hidden were so much more easily exposed there. 'I can't.'

'Then you will be nursed in London by Emerald, Lucinda and Beatrice-Maude.'

'No…'

'Starting today.'

The pounding in his temple stopped him from arguing further and as he lay back against his pillows he knew that he was defeated. Closing his eyes, he slept.

Chapter Nine

Eleanor visited Cristo Wellingham on the second afternoon of his confinement. She had slept so badly for the past two nights that she had come to the conclusion some sense of resolution needed to be reached between them. He received her in the drawing room, the look on his face one of astonished surprise.

'You have come alone?'

'Indeed I have, my lord. I realise, of course, that such a thing is more than inappropriate, but I find I have reached the very end of my patience.'

'A difficult place to be,' he returned and gestured her to a sofa in the middle of the room. Today his hair was pulled back into a queue, and the blond looked almost ash. With his jacket cut in the French fashion and braided along one edge, he seemed much less of the English gentleman and far more of the stranger. Sitting in a wing chair opposite, he stretched out his long legs; when he did not speak, Eleanor felt the need to. 'Are you recovered?'

'Completely.' His tone was distant, as if any more questions on the state of his health would be unwelcomed. Still, she was not deterred.

'My reading on the subject of migraines suggests the case to be the exact opposite. Every tome I browsed made mention of a lack of a cure.'

'A visitor to a sick room generally tries to bring more uplifting news, *madame*.'

The shadows beneath his eyes were visible and one still held the remains of redness. Neither a small ailment nor an easy one.

'In truth, I am surprised to see you here at all, Lady Dromorne.'

The beat of her heart was so loud she felt sure that he must hear it. 'I have prayed every morning and night for some guidance on how to handle our…situation. So far no answer has been forthcoming.'

He laughed. 'How fortuitously honest.'

'What is it you want of me?' She looked him straight in the eye.

'Everything.' His tone was sharp, more honed than she had ever heard it, giving Eleanor the feeling that she was a fly who had tripped heedlessly into a well-laid and intricate web. 'I want to know why every time we touch each other it feels as it did in Paris. I want to understand why you say one thing and mean another. I want to learn how a beautiful English girl masquerading as a whore in Paris can turn up in London five years later in the guise of the wife of an Earl three times older than she is.'

Eleanor stood, her head in a spin, but he had risen as well, amber eyes glinting.

'What was in the letter, Eleanor?'

'I told you once before that I had never read it. My grand-father said to deliver it. He said I could trust you. He said you were a good man...'

His laugh was bitter. 'We both know how very wrong he was!' The words lay between them laced with guilt.

'The travesty at the Château Giraudon was not all your fault...'

'You are more than gracious.' Intent tumbled between the cracks of what was truly being said, and his eyes were fierce and predatory. 'After you left I tried to find you.'

'To entice me back into your bed?'

There it was, out and said, the night of her ruin plain between them, remembered in words and not just thoughts, the pull of flesh and the rush of release. No longer hidden. She could do nothing save wait.

'I didn't forget you, Eleanor.'

'Lady Dromorne,' she corrected.

'I didn't forget anything at all about you, Lady Dromorne.' His stillness belied the words, honey soft and languid. Making love with his voice and his eyes and his hands.

The clock on the mantel struck the hour and outside the clatter of hooves on the cobbles could be heard. But here, now, all she felt lodged in her throat and in her stomach.

A magician. A trickster. A man who had been tutored well in the art of loving and in saying things that any woman might want to hear!

She did not move as he reached out and took her hand, his forefinger running along the lines of her inner palm, gently. Barely there! The breath left her body and the room fell away beneath them, the light streaming hot and golden. As she closed her eyes, the stretch of her belly was long as heat seared into quickness.

Mirrors and gauze and the satiny wet folds between her thighs. Rocking. Wanting. Hours when she had forgotten time and only lived. Desire became a roar as warmth coursed through her, loosening the tight, dry centre with dampness.

His silvered hair and velvet eyes, the smell of masculinity unfettered by age or illness. She revelled in the brown smooth skin on his hands and the strong muscles moving beneath the fabric of his jacket.

'Cristo?'

Even the word was like a salvation, transformed in wonder, spilling from her lips in a lush and radiant question.

Leaning forwards he took her mouth, not gently either, but daring her to resist, a seductive naked want that carried the unsaid promise of all that had been lost between them.

But found again here in the ornate gilded front salon of his London town house, the very Englishness of the décor adding an unreal flavour to what had already been.

She could not stop, could not pull back from his heady vividness. A feast after five years of famine and compromise, her skin sparking as his touch glided along her arm to her throat, reeling her in with only a little force.

Taking everything. Her hat fell away, the ribbons anchoring the bonnet to her shoulders in a drunken uncertainty, his hands through her hair, closer again as all reality was lost against passion.

Like an angel, she thought, as he whispered her name

between the loving, even as the terrible heartbreaking need that had brought her ruin once again surfaced. But she could not care. Would not care.

She placed her hand across his cheek and smiled as he turned into her palm, the warm pulse of his flesh beneath making her nipples stand proud against the silk of her bodice. She knew he saw the promise of her lust and her capitulation, but, shaking his head, he held her against him, heartbeat loud and quick.

'Eleanor, I cannot.'

Only that with the sunshine flooding in and the sound of church bells close! She squeezed her eyes against panic as all she had allowed him became real.

What was she to say now? The glint of her marriage rings caught her eyes as she moved her hand, the small scar Florencia had left there when she had thrown a stick as a toddler, opaque above them.

A wife and a mother who would chance it all away on the promise of lust? She could not even raise her eyes to look at him. Guilt and shame and humiliation all wrapped in stupidity, and the thought that she could be so guileless twice was barely comprehensible.

Cristo stepped back towards the window, trying to assert some sort of control on the situation. No one had ever made him feel the way Eleanor Westbury did. Frustrated. Furious. Desperate. He wanted to drown in her pale eyes and feel the satin smoothness of her skin again. Wanted to lie beside her under an English sun for all the hours that he needed to dull the urgency that had built up inside him.

But he couldn't. A husband stood between them and a whole night's worth of loving that should never have happened.

She did not glance at him once as she rearranged her hat, the brim of it tilted so that it shaded her face from his.

Lord help him! For just a moment, when she had arrived alone, the world was exactly as it should have been before it had skewed into something less tenable.

He needed to tell her how he felt, but for the life of him he could not quite work it out.

Leave your husband and stay with me for ever! Risk the ire of society. Be banned entirely from proper company.

As he was thinking Eleanor began to speak. 'My husband is a principled man of high moral fortitude and unequalled fairness.' The timbre of her voice had risen, almost desperate.

'A Samaritan, then?' In the light of what had happened he should have been kinder.

'Indeed.'

He hated the glint of tears in her eyes. If he had been less scrupulous, he might have reached forwards then and thrown all caution to the wind, taken her upstairs to his room and damned any repercussions. But he had done this once before, and look where that had got them both.

When he did not speak she walked to the door and let herself out. Cristo counted each step that she took across the tiled floor of his foyer as Milne saw to her exit.

Eleanor's hands fisted as she climbed into the carriage waiting for her around the corner. Had Milne recognised her? Had the old butler known her as the woman he had shepherded from the room in the Château Giraudon, with the luridly coloured gypsy skirt swirling around her ankles and an unmade bed left behind? She could barely credit the danger she had allowed herself to be subjected to and the fact that the servant had not seemed to know her was no reason at all to let her guard down.

The truth shattered into fragments. Not quite this or quite that, but an amalgam. Eleanor remembered her father's suicide the year after her brother's death. Her mother had died eighteen months later in a carriage accident with a man who had a reputation for having a way with older women. Her maternal grandfather had denied such rumour, of course, as they sat in the big house after the funeral, but she had seen the look in his eyes that suggested otherwise, and the need for care given that they were the last surviving members of a family that luck had deserted.

Her own youth had been sandwiched between falsities and now here they were again, hemming her into all that she had never thought to become. Well, she could not let them. She would not allow herself to be alone with Cristo Wellingham again. Ever. Cradling the cross she often wore at her neck, she made the promise to herself before turning to look at the people on the busy streets outside and dreaded the Wellingham weekend that she had said she would attend in three days' time.

Honour Baxter arrived less than an hour after Eleanor had left, and she looked neither relaxed nor happy.

'You watch Lady Dromorne like a lover might, Cristo,

a dangerous tendency given the power of her name and of yours.'

He stayed still. Honour was no fool, despite the rather frivolous appearance she presented to the world, as he well knew from her Paris days, before she had made her way to England and married.

'I think she wants you, too.'

He turned as she said it.

'There is a child, of course, and the Earl of Dromorne would never countenance any threat to his daughter's happiness and stability.'

Shock rendered him speechless. A child? Eleanor had a child? He had heard no word of one at all.

'How old is she?'

Honour shrugged her shoulders. 'Nearly five. A girl who is rarely seen out in public. Florencia is her name.'

Nearly five.

Florencia.

If Eleanor had been fertile at Giraudon, then conception would have been the easiest thing in the world.

Nearly five. He counted back. Was the child his? Could he be a father? The heavy beat of his heart vibrated in his ears and he shut his eyes as he sat on the sofa.

'Are you quite well, Cristo? Should I call someone?'

'No, please don't.' His voice sounded like the string of some instrument tuned to the very last of its strength, a breaking point just waiting to happen as loss welled in his throat. Florencia. Even her name was beautiful. Swallowing, he made himself listen to Honour's next words.

'London has rules that would be ludicrous in the more

passionate arena of Paris. What is acceptable there would not be here and there are many unwed and beautiful English girls just waiting for you to notice them, women without the ties of children and husbands. Let me introduce you to these girls of good family and unblemished name.'

He nodded, simply because to do otherwise would have incited question. His glance took in the clock on the mantel that showed up the hour of four and he wondered what outings little girls and their mothers went on in London at such a time. The park? The shops? The library on Bond Street?

When the hell had Eleanor met Martin Dromorne? He longed to ask Honour, but sense stopped him. He felt like he had at eighteen, abandoned by his family. No safety net. Unsettled. The very room swam with a hundred questions and just as many answers and everything was dangerous.

Florencia. Derived from the city of Florence in Italy? He listened as Honour prattled on about a list of possible candidates suitable in the marriage stakes.

Florencia. The word turned in his mind as Honour gave high praise to the three débutantes shortlisted in her attempt at matchmaking.

Florencia. His? A daughter conceived in lust in the high rooflines above Paris? If that was true, where had Eleanor birthed the child? Here? In France? Ruined from a husbandless pregnancy?

What of Martin Dromorne? Did he know this daughter was not his? Had she met him soon afterwards, perhaps, seizing the opportunity for redemption that marriage offered? Or was all he thought mere conjecture based on a groundless hope?

Eleanor and Florencia.

He dared not ask Honour another thing about either of them as a servant came in with a pot of tea and the conversation turned to more general things.

Taris arrived about ten minutes after Honour had departed. His man Bates was with him, though after seeing his master into the room he slipped out of it. His brother had a bright yellow flower threaded through his lapel.

'You look festive?'

Taris lifted his hand up and smiled. 'This is the handiwork of my oldest son, who is inclined to mischief. His twin brother enjoys the school lessons and yet all Alfred can think of is to escape his and head for the gardens.'

'Ahh, the danger of comparisons. I never thought that you would make them.'

'When you are a parent you do many things that you had not thought you would. But out of love, you understand. Only out of that.'

Parenthood! In the light of Honour's visit the raw nerve of hope was exposed and Cristo was glad that his brother could not read his expression.

'Ashe said that he had been to visit you and so I decided to do the same. He said that you seemed pleased to see him.'

'Sickness has a habit of making one re-evaluate the usefulness of family.'

'So cynical?' Laughter rang around the room. 'Our father always swore that you were stubborn.'

'And did he ever tell you why?' Cristo had suddenly had

enough of all the secrecy. 'Did he ever let you know that I was not entirely a Wellingham?'

When Taris's face came up to his own with a slight flush Cristo suddenly knew that he had.

'Alice never blamed him for his indiscretion. She told us that as she took her last breath. She also said that you were a gift she was meant to have. She kept track of you at Giraudon through your man Milne, you realise. The old valet at Falder was his brother and she never let him go.'

Cristo swore. What other confidences was he destined to hear this morning? A child who might be his? A mother who had never stopped loving him? Two brothers who had known he was not a full-blooded son of Falder and had treated him as one anyway? A feeling he had forgotten he knew was again budding. No longer alone. No longer just him against the world.

Shared secrets and trust, and beside a brother whose eyes saw what others never did, and with all the unexpected twists and turns Cristo found himself talking.

'When I left England I thought to have seen the last of it.'

'What changed your mind?'

His hands opened and then he smiled, because of course Taris would not see the gesture. 'When the wild anger died there was only loneliness to replace it.'

'Beatrice thinks that there might be a woman.'

'She told you that?'

'She thinks the woman to be Martin Westbury's wife, Lady Eleanor Dromorne?'

Cristo stayed silent.

'The mistakes of youth can come back to haunt even the most circumspect. The thing that I cannot quite determine is where your shared history took place.'

'I met her in Paris five years ago.'

'Before she was married?'

'Yes.'

'But you made no effort to take the relationship further?'

'I think it had gone the furthest it could go.'

A ripe curse greeted this outburst.

'If I could go back I would do things differently. In my defence, I might add that I did not know she was an English lady.'

'Surely you could tell that by her clothes and her accent?'

'She wasn't wearing any clothes and she was speaking Provençal French.'

'Lord, so that was why she fainted at the theatre? Does Martin Westbury know of any of this?'

'I am certain that he doesn't. He didn't seem to want to kill me when we met at the Baxters'.'

Taris picked the marigold from his buttonhole and the stringent smell of it filled the air as he fiddled with the petals. Bright yellow pollen dusted the back of one hand.

'Everyone has their battles. Martin Westbury, for example, is so ill some say it won't be long before he loses his fight against whatever it is that ails him. Eleanor Westbury may then need a man who would not disappoint her.'

'I doubt that she would trust me again.'

'Well, that all depends. You can let your past mistakes

define you or transform you. A wise man might take the latter option.'

Cristo breathed out. 'I thought she was a prostitute brought to my room. With the amount of brandy she had consumed, she could not tell me otherwise and by then I had discovered that she was a virgin.'

'An inauspicious beginning?' Dark amber eyes looked straight at him and Cristo began to laugh at the absurdity of a word that only Taris might get away with.

'Very.'

'There are rumours you worked for the Foreign Office in Paris?'

'In the capacity of one who would safeguard the interests of England, you understand, for even in peacetime there are those who might undermine the relationship between the two countries. Smitherton sent trainers down to the château I owned in Paris.'

'A difficult job, I should imagine.'

'Sometimes it was.'

'And is it still?'

'No. I have left the service.'

'For retirement into peaceful obscurity?'

When Cristo laughed Taris joined in and for the first time in a long while the ghosts of past misunderstandings faded.

Chapter Ten

Martin still insisted on her going to the Wellinghams', a weekend house party at Beaconsmeade that would mean them leaving early on Friday evening and returning on Sunday night.

With the dresses fitted and the girls and Diana excited, Eleanor looked for ways in which she could turn down the invitation without inviting comment.

Consequently she took to her bed on Thursday afternoon with a stomach ailment that had her refusing the night meal. She did not expect Martin's visit, however, later that evening and was caught reading a book and eating from a box of chocolates that Florencia had bought for her on a trip into town with Diana a few weeks back.

'For a woman suffering from nausea you look surprisingly well.' Tonight he looked better than he had in many months.

She stayed silent.

'Is there some reason that the Beaconsmeade outing is worrying you?'

She decided to brazen it out. 'Florencia will miss me—'
He didn't let her finish.

'I am here and I have already told you that I should like
to have a few days with my daughter for company. It is not
often that I see her alone.'

Eleanor nodded, at a loss now to keep on with her arguments.

'You are young, my dear, and it is important that you enjoy
these sorts of things. I know Diana will be lost without you
if you don't attend, for she has made the fact known to me.
Besides, I thought you admired the Wellingham women!'

'I do.'

'Then what keeps you from going? I know the dresses are
finished and the girls have said how lovely yours looked.'

Eleanor's glance went to the wardrobe where her new
gowns were shrouded in calico. Shoes and cloaks and bags
and hats were in the boxes beneath them. All readied for
the carriage ride south into Kent.

She wanted to say that she was afraid. She wanted to
shout it out so that he might actually hear her. Afraid of
herself and of her reactions! Afraid others might notice or
that Cristo Wellingham himself might notice or that the
feelings she held deep inside her would never be returned
as he made a play for one of the other younger and prettier
girls present.

But she could say none of this because to voice even a
little of it would be to betray Martin altogether, and he had
no idea at all that Cristo Wellingham was the Frenchman
who had taken her into his bed in Paris. So she stayed silent,
smiling as he took her hand and turned it palm upwards.

'I want you to go and enjoy this chance, Eleanor. I want you to be happy again.'

That threw her. 'I am not sad.'

'Preoccupied, then. Lately you have been different.'

The truth settled around them. His truth and her own at odds, but she could not hurt him with the kindness in his eyes and the history between them.

'Perhaps we should go away, Martin, far from London, to the hills up north or to the sea on the south coast. The change of air could be good for you after all...'

He stopped her before she went any further. 'I doubt that I could manage a big shift of circumstance and I enjoy watching the traffic go by from my upstairs bedroom. It always makes me feel a part of the world.'

'Of course.' The chance to simply decamp from the city was not an option and so she nodded, knowing that in her capitulation she was risking everything and equally as determined not to.

Beaconsmeade was a large Palladian-style country house situated on rising ground with lawns stretching up to it and parkland as far as the eye could see below.

The party was in full swing when they arrived as a number of other carriages had come at the same time as they had.

With servants and horses and people and luggage the circular drive was awash with movement and Eleanor did not see Beatrice-Maude Wellingham until the very last moment.

'I am so pleased that you could come,' the older woman said as she took her hand in her own. Looking about quickly to see if any other Wellinghams were in close proximity, she relaxed when she saw that they were not.

'I have placed you on the second floor in the blue suite of rooms. The girls are in the larger dark blue room and their mother in the smaller one with an adjoining door. You will have the light blue room a little farther down the corridor. I hope this will be to your liking.'

'Oh, I am certain it will all be lovely,' Eleanor replied, wishing as she said it that she might have been allotted a shared room with her sister-in-law as a further safety.

'The Duke and Duchess of Carisbrook will be coming presently, but Cristo cannot be down until the morning. Lady Lucinda has arrived already with the Henshaws and the Beauchamps.'

'A full house, then,' Diana chirped in, standing at Eleanor's elbow now with glitter-bright excitement in her eyes.

Beatrice-Maude smiled. 'We will have some of the local families here, too, and their offspring for the evening meal. I am certain your daughters will enjoy their company.'

Sophie and Margaret nodded politely and Eleanor could almost read their thoughts as they did so. It was not the local boys that the girls had set their hearts on at all, but Cristo Wellingham with his silvered hair and secrets. She had been regaled all the way down with his wealth and his prowess at fighting and the château that he was reputed to own in Paris.

Eleanor had longed to ask how they had found out these things, but didn't because any interest might be misinterpreted and she had no desire for her nieces to perceive a curiosity they would question.

Even now Sophie risked good manners and broached a topic of her own.

'Will Lord Cristo be coming alone, madam?'

'He will, Miss Cameron, although I am not certain whether he will spend the night here or not.'

Better and better, Eleanor thought and smiled properly for the first time in days. Twelve hours at most to be in his company and then that would be the end of it. Apart from a few moments of polite and general conversation what really could go wrong? A clap of thunder and the beginning of a shower of rain sent them hurrying inside.

She should never have got on this stupid horse, she thought the next day as it again took the lead and tried to head into the thinning forest away from the track.

'Keep up, Eleanor,' Diana called from in front. 'Use the whip and then it won't tarry.'

All morning she had been struggling with the steed, and though the whole party had made great allowances for her and had slowed their pace considerably, the beautiful wide tracks in the forest had become too much of a temptation and they had gone ahead to wait for her at the end of the pathway.

The skin beneath the gloves on Eleanor's hands was beginning to ache with the constant tugging and the rain threatening yesterday was again in sight, bands of dark grey clouds looming overhead.

Suddenly she had just had enough, and, dismounting, she determined to lead her horse on foot.

'You go on, Diana.' Her shout made Diana stop, caught

between the outlines of her disappearing daughters and Eleanor's distress.

'Should I stay with you?'

'No. Sophie and Margaret may need you and I think I have had enough of riding. Besides, I can see the house from here so shall make my own way back.' The countryside of Kent was beautiful and in the places where the trees did not stand she saw fields in the distance and the house of Beaconsmeade on the ridge behind.

There was a short silence and then acquiescence. 'Well, if you are certain...'

'I am.'

'I'll send back a servant to accompany you when I catch them up.'

When Eleanor nodded Diana used her whip hard against the flanks of her mount and was gone, the noises of the small forest closing in again around her.

Silence in a natural way. She felt elated by her solitude, something she rarely had in London. Removing her hat, she loosened her hair so that it fell in waves down her back, the length of it almost touching her waist.

Cristo Wellingham had not come. She had thought he would be there in the morning when she had gone down for breakfast, but he had been delayed and was not now expected to arrive till well after luncheon.

Her eyes went to the watch in her pocket. The servant that Diana had spoken of had not appeared and she wondered why. Almost twelve o'clock now. If she tarried a little and explored a few of the paths that went off this one, she might be away for a while longer. Her thoughts calculated how long she could be away without raising any alarm and she decided thirty minutes or so might not go amiss. The path to her left looked fairly robust and flat and the trees around it thinner than any of the other tracks. If she turned off here?

Marking her exit with a stone she gathered a few of the wildflowers around it and placed them on the top. When she returned to this point she would know to proceed left. Glancing up and down the well-used track once more just to see that no servant had been sent back to help her, she walked into the dimness, leading the horse, and her shape was lost in the shadows.

'She said she would go directly back and I watched her turn for Beaconsmeade.'

Lady Diana Cameron, Westbury's sister, was speaking and the shrill panic in her voice was easily heard. Outside the weather was worsening and the clouds threatening all morning had finally broken into rain.

Cristo stepped into the pandemonium, having set foot in Beaconsmeade only ten minutes prior.

'Lady Dromorne has not been seen since she turned back from our ride at around twelve o'clock. Her sister-in-law was certain that she said she was returning here and the house was able to be seen from the track.' Beatrice looked a little harried as the parlour clock struck three.

'Have people been sent out to look for her?' Cristo felt his own sense of alarm as they nodded.

'Asher went out an hour ago with some servants but hasn't returned, though I am certain he will find her.'

'I'll take Demeter and see if I can be of some use.' The property was new to him, too, so he asked for directions that would lead him to the area used for the morning's ride.

Half an hour later Cristo found a rock that had been newly overturned on the edge of a small track leading farther into the forest. When he dismounted he noticed a few wilting flowers lying on the side of it, the wind having pushed them there out of the way.

Kneeling, he looked for other things. A broken twig and grass that was worn.

Here. She had left the track here. Setting the stone in the middle of the trail as a message to alert the others, he turned his horse into the shadows.

She should never have thought of such an idea, because with all the turns in the pathway she was now well and truly lost and the horse had dug in its feet and refused to move another inch. Goodness, it was already nearly four o'clock and Diana must be frantic by now.

'Stupid horse,' she said to him as she sat on a log near a small stream. 'Stupid, stupid horse.' The words brought his head up and he looked directly at her, interest written in his soft brown eyes; because of that she laughed, feeling vaguely mean about growling at an animal who just wanted an easy life.

If she left him here and walked on alone would he be all right? Would he follow? She decided to try it, disappearing around a corner and waiting to see if the steed would move.

He didn't.

Returning, she grabbed at his reins and tried again to drag him.

'You cannot possibly wish to stay here all by yourself and, besides, it is about to rain.' As she said it the clouds burst open, sending a downpour across the small glade and pinning her curls to her head and clothes.

'Now look what has happened,' she continued, 'and it is all your fault. Come on. We have to get home before it becomes dark.'

A noise a little way away made her stiffen. Something was coming their way. Some forest predator? Finding a substantial piece of wood near her feet, she lifted it and went to stand at the head of the stubborn horse.

'It will be perfectly all right. Don't you worry, I will make certain that nothing eats you.'

She hated the tremble she could hear in her voice and the ache of fright banding her stomach.

It was coming closer through the trees, she determined, along the path she had turned off a moment or so back. Her fingers tightened about the wood.

She was talking to the horse? Telling him it was all his fault and that she would allow nothing to eat him, a stick in her hand of such old timber that it would break into pieces at the very first contact.

If he wasn't so angry he might have smiled, but the afternoon was darkening with rain, and Eleanor Westbury was hardly wearing anything to warm her save a thin jacket and a piece of lace around her neck. Her hair was everywhere and very wet. If he had not found her, what then…? The very thought of it made him scowl as he strode into the clearing.

Cristo Wellingham was here? In the glade far from anyone with the fading light about them and anger in his eyes. She did not lower the piece of wood, but held it as a barrier between them.

'People in trouble generally don't hit their rescuers.'

His eyes were amber brittle as she tried to stop the shaking that had overcome her.

'Your sister-in-law is, as we speak, imagining you to be in all sorts of trouble.' His glance took in her sorry-looking mount with a singular understanding of its intractability.

'How did you find me?'

'The stone and some flowers! At least you thought to do that.'

'You walked in?'

'No. My bay is tethered a few minutes back. I heard your voice and followed the sound.'

He came forwards, but did not stop when he reached her, leaning down instead to check the saddle of her horse.

'This is the problem,' he said after a moment, disengaging a sprig of prickles. 'They sometimes get burred on the skin and hurt with any movement or pressure.'

Straightening, he removed his hat and dusted it against the pale brown of his riding breeches. He was dressed today as an English country gentleman and Eleanor wondered if he would ever stop surprising her. Silence was punctuated only by the call of birds settling in the trees and by the trill of the river water a few yards away.

'I arrived at Beaconsmeade as the rescue parties were being dispatched,' he said finally. 'I am glad it was me who found you.'

The last words were said in a different tone from the others and the skin on her arms rose in response. Pure and utter awareness, no pretence in any of it.

'Glad?'

'It gives us some time to talk.'

'Talk?' The heat in her was fiery red and she wondered if he could see the blush of it in her face.

'Unless you would want more.' He reached out as though to touch her and she stepped back. Not trusting his touch. Not trusting him.

Today he wore a ring on his little finger, the man in Paris creeping back in slow measures here. 'Honour Baxter said that you had a daughter.'

'I do.' She made herself look at him, straight in the eye, as though they spoke of the weather or the lie of the land or some other insignificant thing. Only bravado and confidence would throw him off track.

'Could I meet her?'

'Why?'

'She is almost five and I hear that she is a fair child with dark eyes.'

'And you think because of it she could be yours?' She laughed. 'My mother was a beauty of some note and her colouring was the same.'

'Your husband looks too ill to father a child.'

'Now, perhaps, that might be the case. But back then…'
The ending was left unsaid.

'Honour says the child is named Florencia?'

'Martin and I lived in Florence for a good few years before coming back to England. It was in compliment to the city that she was named such.' Pushing the boundaries further, she dredged up sympathy. 'I am very sorry if you are disappointed or if you had imagined…'

Shrugging the sentiment away, he was closer now, so close she could feel the breath of him against her face when he spoke. Yet still he did not touch.

'Is your husband kind, Eleanor?'

Martin's name here under a canopy of trees, here in the wind as the day turned into dusk and the leaves rustled.

'Of course.'

He smiled at that, the corners of his eyes creasing and showing up the depth of colour in his skin. Not a man who was trapped indoors, nor a man whose muscles and bone were wasting daily. She shook the thought away and concentrated on other things.

'In Paris I was a fool to let you go so easily.' The velvet in his eyes was lighter against the low sun, the colour of dark brandy with fire behind it.

Tears were close. She could feel them pooling, at the waste of it all and at the yearning that she could no longer deny.

She knew she should turn away this moment, now, or at the very least direct the conversation into a more indifferent topic. She should stake her claim on being a sensible woman, a prudent woman, a woman who had no thought for the passion consuming her.

But when he reached out she let him touch her and when he brought her knuckles to his lips and kissed the back of them she felt his tongue like the sharp blade of a razor drawing her blood into shivers.

'Do you feel that?' The question was fierce. 'Do you, Eleanor. Feel that?'

'No.' She could not let him speak any longer, could not allow him to say the words that marked a truth.

'No?' He laid his other hand across the jutting flesh of her bosom, feeling the beat of her heart. The rain wet his hand as she looked down, cold against warmth. She almost expected to see steam.

'Eleanor. Whatever this is…?'

'Is between us,' she finished and laid a finger on his lips against further words, tracing the line of them, carefully. She felt in his constraint a terrible desperation.

'I failed you once and I should not have….'

Once! Her other hand was held rigidly against her side, gripped into a fist as she thought of the tiny grave at the chapel in Aix-en-Provence planted with spring bulbs because they were all she could leave untended.

Not now. Not now. The guilt that rode her dreams nightly opened into full bloom, reaching down into the very core of her heart. Swallowing, she made herself relax as puzzlement crept into his eyes.

'I would not hurt you, Eleanor.'

She blanched at the pitch of need so clearly heard and the distance that held them apart lessened. Closer and closer as his hands tightened on her shoulders, drawing her in.

Six inches and then her breasts flattened against his chest, finding home.

No child. No husband. Only him. Only him with his silvered wet hair and his magical mouth and his hand around her head tilting her into more, their breath heavy and torrid as she matched his desire with her own.

Mine. Again. Amongst the trees and the oncoming darkness and the call of the birds as they settled for the night, watching. Watching a dam break in the circle of flesh, tipping into utter need, his grip tightening in her hair as an anchor, no breath or ease or quiet exploration. Only five years of apartness and ten thousand hours of regret. Only the sweet rush of his breath and the clamp of passion that knotted her body from tip to toe into some other unknown force, giving back all that she was getting, opening to him so that he could come in, deeper, closer, the feel of him against her body so very, very right.

'I want you...'

His voice was strained, no longer distant, no longer indifferent, only pain within them.

'I am married.'

Martin. She tried to bring his face to her thoughts, but couldn't. Cristo smelt of soap and musk and strength and the memory of Paris flooded back, of arching into delight and finding the hidden notes of pleasure in the slightest of caresses. Potent memory, honed with a celibacy that had taken all her passionate years since, month by month by month.

Sweat dripped beneath the raindrops as ecstasy boiled, and then the seconds ran out under the urgent shadow of lust and she surrendered to the sheer promise of what was offered. Her toes arched in her boots and her head tipped back, his hands steadying her.

Even then she could not feel shame or contrition. Nay, all she could feel was the throbbing release through the very core of her body, untying all the knots and the pressure and leaving a freedom that she remembered from only once before.

'I love you.'

Had she whispered it? Please God, let it not be so!

He broke away and laid her face against his chest, his heart wild-beating fast.

'Damn. Others are coming.'

She could not hear a sound.

'They will be here inside two minutes.'

She was glad he did not look back at her as he walked away.

Chapter Eleven

Asher Wellingham and his men came into the glade by foot and along the same route that Cristo had taken.

'Her steed was lame,' Cristo said from his place on the other side of the horse. He sounded normal, indifferent, the kiss of a moment back a long-forgotten thing. 'You found the marker, I guess.'

The Duke of Carisbrook nodded. Up close, Eleanor could see a familial resemblance that had nothing to do with the shape of nose or mouth or face. It was menace and danger that entwined the Wellingham brothers as well as height and darkness of eye. Both looked at each other with a glance that held a myriad questions beneath the polite exterior.

'Are you quite well, Lady Dromorne?' Asher Wellingham addressed her now, as he picked up a stick and threw it into the undergrowth.

'Very well, thank you, your Grace. I walked along the path and was lost…'

'But now you are found.' The sentiment was not quite said in the way Eleanor would have expected it and when she turned to Cristo she saw him send a flinty glance in warning to his oldest brother.

The Duke laughed.

'Is your mount able to be ridden at all, Lady Dromorne?'

All she could do was nod.

'Then if you will ride behind me, Cristo will bring up the rear. Would that meet with your approval?'

Such formality in the middle of nowhere was confusing, but she was pleased for the proposed distance.

Cristo dried himself off in the bedroom he had been given and one that reminded him of his own childhood chamber at Falder. Even the fabric on the bed was similar. Golden. Sheer curtains and French doors along one whole side of the room. But it was the books that caught his attention. His books, title by title, of collections he had begun as a youth. He ran his finger across the spines in wonder. Who had brought these here? Who had cared for them? Hearing footfalls, he turned and Beatrice-Maude swept into his room after a quick and perfunctory knock.

'I hope you do not mind about the books.'

'You took them?'

'Cared for them,' she amended, 'until you should want them back. At Falder they had begun to wilt and I thought if they had been mine I would hope someone should watch over them.'

'Thank you.'

He waited for her to say something else, but she didn't.

'Have you read many?'

She ignored this line of conversation completely.

'Eleanor Westbury is not a woman who would survive being duped. She is young, after all, and her husband of some years is sick...'

'Did Taris send you here?'

'No. I am here because a few weeks ago Lady Dromorne told me that you might defame her character. Given the time you spent alone with her today I wondered if there was indeed some truth in her fear?'

Taris's wife was not a woman to bandy her thoughts around and yet all his training told him that she held the best interests of Eleanor Westbury at heart. He could use a woman like her on his side.

'I knew Eleanor once many years ago in Paris and under another name.'

'How many years?'

'Five.'

The number lay between them coated in question.

'Her daughter...'

'Is five.' He finished the sentence for her and leant against the wall, the rushing in his head alerting him to another onslaught of his ailment.

'God.' Two attacks in two weeks. They never came this close.

'Are you quite well?'

'Very.'

'Your eyes are turning red even as we speak.'

He let go of the wall and just made it to the bed. Once horizontal, he felt immeasurably better.

'Could you do something for me, Beatrice-Maude?' It was the first time he had called her by her name.

She nodded.

'Could you let the party below know that I have been called away to town and that I send my very sincerest apologies? I need peace and quiet, and that will stop people coming up to see me. Could you also tell Lady Dromorne that I will call on her in town this week.'

'Indeed, brother-in-law, I think it would be most wise if I did just that.'

He frowned as she let herself out and shut the door behind her.

I love you. Eleanor had whispered the words beneath her breath, but he had heard them plainly. Lord, he thought as he laid his arm against his face to block out the last bands of light, his hand fisting against pain. She was a wife and a mother and a woman who would not court the danger of ruin. But there were secrets in her eyes and in her words that could be there because of him and her sadness here in England simply broke his heart.

He had left and gone back to London. In haste. Eleanor knew exactly why he had.

I love you. So, so unwise. Why had she said it? She knew the answer as soon as she asked herself the question.

Because the last waves of lust had still been within her, reforming the way she looked at herself, a woman who might enjoy the acts between a man and a woman with a singular abandon. Young. Free. Sensual. No longer scared and careful, the restraints of manners and culture pulling her into greyness.

Today with Cristo Wellingham she had felt powerful and

true. To herself. A woman who could not wait another five years to feel…something.

Beatrice-Maude was looking at her now as she sipped at a cup of tea from the breakfast table.

'Cristo has been unfortunately recalled to town and he has asked me to give his most sincere apologies. I should imagine that there is much to do when one is newly back in a country one has not lived in for years. He did, however, promise to visit your family when he was able. Mayhap we could all come.'

Her words brought a smile to Taris Wellingham's face as he watched her.

A love match.

It was said their union was such, but in a town that spawned a thousand marriages a year, few were of that ilk.

Regret surfaced in an unexpected deluge as she thought of her own marriage. Martin had protected her, but never touched her. Perhaps it was his illness or his age, or the fact that when he had first met her she had been so very near to death, and a pattern had formed. Eleanor remembered the hospital in Aix and the blood and the tiny twin who had been left in the cemetery of the Chapel de la Francis, his body marked with a simple white stone.

Paris.

She had called him that. A strong name. A warrior's name. The name of the beautiful Trojan prince who had stolen Helen from Menelaus, and the name of the city in which he had been conceived. The hair on the crown of his tiny head had been pure silver. His father's son. She had never known the colour of his eyes because it had been a full week until the fever had left her and another two before she could even speak. The anger in her solidified and she hated the thick thump of her grief.

So alone.

If she had been braver she might have saved him…in a bigger city…with better attendants…

Shaking her head, she came back into the moment, leaving behind fury, but the light had gone out of her evening and all she wanted to do was to depart Beaconsmeade and go home to Florencia.

He dreamed that night of the ship he had taken when he left England. The Hell Ship. The Hell Captain. Things done to his body that he had never told anyone, an eighteen-year-old green boy straight out of Cambridge. The sears of whiplashes on his back ached in memory.

The canker of secrecy had eaten him up, piece by piece, catapulting him into the underworld of Paris with an easy transition.

Wrong. It was all wrong.

I love you. Eleanor's whispered words. The first right thing in his whole damn life.

Feeling the movement of somebody else in the room, he opened his eyes. Ashe sat above him.

Cristo knew he had heard his secrets as he turned away, anger leaving only heartbeat in his ears.

'Smitherton got to you, didn't he? At Cambridge? God, and he promised me that he wouldn't. That's what you were doing in Paris?'

'I could have left.'

'No.' The word was rough with fury. 'No one ever leaves until their very soul is gone. It's the way he works it.'

'How do you know?'

'Because he got to me first and it was years before I could loosen the grip of it all. Wasted lonely years that taught me only how to hate.'

The light breeze from outside billowed the gauze curtains into a soft cloud, a summer night in the heart of Kent so far from the paths that they both had travelled.

'Buy the damn Graveson property, Cris, and come home.' His brother's hand lay across his arm.

'My lawyers got it yesterday. That's why I was late down to Beaconsmeade.'

Laughter lit Asher's eyes, the amber in them so very like his own. 'This calls for a toast.' He filled two glasses with lemonade and handed one over.

'To family.'

With a headache pounding his temples, Cristo smiled. 'Everything has a pattern, Ashe. And Graveson is the very first link of the chain.'

An hour later when Asher had left, Cristo sat up on the side of his bed, watching the candle on the side table burn.

I love you.

If he had had even a little bit of decency in him he would pack up his things and return to the Château Giraudon. Away from temptation, delivered from evil.

He could only hurt her. Then he amended. He could only hurt them both with his reappearance and this damnable attraction simmering between them.

I love you.

He had said the words to himself a hundred times. I love you enough to leave my husband? I love you enough to risk my daughter's name? I love you so much I would throw caution to the wind and follow you to the edge of the world?

Reality stung and the ache in his heart was a signpost to a more virtuous truth. He should leave her to the life she was living and a family who had taken her as one of their own.

His name held only a little of what Martin Dromorne offered her, dogged as it was by scandal and mayhem. Oh, granted his brothers had gone out of their way to make him a son of Falder, but even that truth was cankered.

A half-brother. A bastard child. The son of a mother whom he had killed in childbirth and had been sent away summarily, no place in the hearts of her relatives for the reminder of such tragedy!

It was Alice who had saved him. Alice with her kind eyes and an open heart that had never once wavered in its love. And in the end he had failed her as well with his wild anger and bad choices.

He seldom allowed himself the time to wallow in self-pity but tonight, with the circumstances heavily weighed against him, he did. He frowned at the notion of a virtuous withdrawal from London for he knew he would never do it.

Fighting for what he wanted to have and hold was far more his style, but he would need to be careful and prudent.

'Bide your time,' he whispered and the candle caught the breath of the words and flickered.

'I love you,' he added and this time the flame barely moved.

* * *

Eleanor spent the next few days pleading tiredness when anyone suggested an outing. Even the park seemed dangerous, an open space that might bring her face to face with the one man in the world she could no longer even bear to think about.

I love you.

She screwed up her eyes and swore beneath her breath, the silence in the blue drawing room making the memory worse. Why had she said it? Had he heard? Was he laughing with a friend at this very moment somewhere in a club in London as he remembered her ill-advised confession?

Certainly Cristo Wellingham had not contacted her at all and Sophie and Margaret lamented the fact that he was not at the dances that they had chosen to attend. Disappeared. Gone. She hoped with all of her heart that he had said nothing about her to Lady Beatrice-Maude or the Duchess of Carisbrook.

'You need to get some colour back in your cheeks, Lainie.' Diana had entered the chamber with her small basket of tapestry threads and a pair of spectacles. 'We could go shopping if you wish, for I have some colours I need to procure,' and held up her stitchwork. Eleanor saw the picture to be a Christmas one, a hearth dressed in gold and silver and the full moon in the window to one side.

'It's for Geoffrey's mother,' Diana said as she saw her looking. 'She asked me last year if I would do one and I was determined to begin it early. You could all come up to Edinburgh for the Yule season. Martin always loved Scotland.'

'I am not certain…'

'Because of his health?'

It was the first time his sister had even mentioned the topic and Eleanor nodded.

'You need to get out more, Eleanor. At your age I was—' She stopped. 'Are you crying?'

'No. Of course not.' The tears that welled in her eyes were dashed away on the material of her sleeve as Eleanor turned to the window. 'It's just sometimes I think I should be a better wife to your brother.'

'Nonsense.' Diana laid down her sewing and came to put her arms around her. 'He could not have wished for a more caring helpmate. But he is a good thirty years older than you, Lainie, and sometimes that must be difficult.' She paused briefly. 'Is it morning sickness, perhaps, that makes you so up and down, for lately you have seemed very emotional?'

For a second Eleanor could not quite work out the change of conversation.

Morning sickness? My God, Diana thought she could be pregnant? She shook her head vigorously, and her sister-in-law retreated a little.

'It was just after you fainted at the theatre and I thought… But of course not! Martin hardly has enough energy for the daytime, let alone the night. Besides, another child with his problems…' She let her words tail off.

Another child?

The whitewashed hospital walls with the small effigy of the Mother Mary built into a shelf filled with dried rosemary. Bile rose in her mouth. She had hated the smell of rosemary ever since. Cloying. Smothering. The doctor had been a man of high principle and he had known she was unmarried. As such, he had not even attempted to hide his condemnation when she had delivered a child who had failed to take a breath. Even his words had been ones of blame.

'Every babe needs a father and this is the Lord's way of making certain of it. Be thankful for your reprieve.'

Be thankful for your reprieve. The words still had the propensity to make her feel sick. He had smiled as he said it before placing her baby into a basin on the floor and leaving it there. Cold. Untended.

No cuddles or gentleness. No prayer for an innocent soul as it went into Heaven. Eleanor had tried to say the communion herself, but the incantation had been muddled, and the red wash of her own blood had left her mute and terrified.

Paris. Lost in guilt and censure and fear.

'Lainie? Are you quite all right? I shouldn't pry, of course, and you have the perfect right to tell me to mind my own business.'

Shaking her head, the anger twisted back into some workable thing. She had had much practice in tethering it, after all, though her ill-advised confession to Cristo in the forest had changed things somewhat and all for the worse.

'I love you.'

What if she had stayed with Cristo in Paris as his mistress, would her son have lived? If she had gone to him and told him and pleaded her case? Their case. An eighteen-year-old girl in limbo in a land that was not home.

Choices, good and bad, and now other decisions, the stakes rising again because of her daughter!

'Ever since Beaconsmeade you have been distracted. I should never have left you alone in the woods, of course, and I kick myself for following my daughters.'

'No. The fault was mine. Exploring the pathway was such a silly idea.'

'Indeed, it was one I could not for the life of me understand. You are usually such a cautious girl, Lainie, which is probably a characteristic my brother saw in you that appealed the most for, God bless him, he is exactly the same.'

Chapter Twelve

Eleanor led Florencia around the park on her daughter's tiny pony enjoying the summer day. She had not heard a word from Cristo Wellingham in well over a week and for that she was glad, the respite from the constant fear of seeing him lessening her worry.

'When I am bigger, Mama, I will buy the very best, best horse and race it around the park.'

Her father's daughter, for all had heard the rumours that Cristo Wellingham was in town to select prime horse-flesh.

'Not too fast, darling, for there are always people in these places.' Lord, Eleanor thought grimly. Already I am clipping her wings just as my mother clipped mine.

'All I want is a pet, Mama. Even just a kitten…' There was a tone in her voice that was sullen, a tone she had heard more often of late when Florencia addressed her—almost five and needing the boundaries only a strong father might offer.

'Excuse me, ma'am.' A young boy stood before her with

a letter in his hand. 'The man said that I was to give you this.'

'The man. What man?' For one moment she thought perhaps Cristo Wellingham had sent it and looked around, her cheeks flushing with the thought that he could be close.

'Oh, he has gone already. He paid me a shilling.' The coin caught the sunlight as he opened his palm.

'Who is he, Mama?' Florencia had watched them, this unusual occurrence widening her eyes and when Eleanor turned again the boy had rushed off, his back seen between a line of oaks farther off in the park.

Slitting the envelope with her finger, she opened out the single sheet of paper, her heart contracting in horror as she read the message inside.

You are the whore from the Château Giraudon. If you want to stay safe leave a hundred pounds in this envelope with the boy waiting outside the instrument shop in Regent Street next Monday morning at ten.

Unsigned, the letter represented everything that she had always feared might happen. Blackmail. Finally. Placing the note in her reticule, she turned the pony for home, ignoring the wails of her irritated daughter.

Two days after she had paid, another letter came. This time directly to her house, sitting in the salver at the front door, the blue of the envelope familiar. Pouncing on complacency.

In her room she understood the danger of paying anything in the first place. This time five hundred pounds was demanded, a sum that even her personal pin money could not hope to conceal. She stuffed the note into the fire burning low in the front salon due to an unseasonably cold day, and watched it go up into flames, each word curling into ash and then cinder.

My God, what on earth should she do? Who could it be writing such things? The paper was expensive and the hand was correct and well formed. A small idea began to crystallise in her brain. Pulling out a sheet of her own stationery, she wrote a plea to the only man who might help her, the only man who would be as implicated as she was in the uncertainty of blackmail.

She hired a hack and waited at the corner of Beak and Regent Street at exactly the hour she had indicated, fear, excitement and discomposure racing through her in equal measures.

Cristo Wellingham would be here at any second, her last foolish confession unanswered between them, and already her body was knotting into the memory of his touch. Taking in breath, she held it, tight, as though in the movement she might harness a longing that came just with the thought of him. Her hands shook in her lap.

And then he was there, dressed today in the finest of his London finery, the white cravat at his throat throwing up the darkness of his skin and eyes. The gloves he removed after he entered the carriage and sat opposite her, his hat joining them on the leather seat.

'Eleanor?' She had forgotten how tall he was and how the smell of him made her want to just breathe in for ever. His hair was pulled back and damp.

'Thank you for coming.' Her voice sounded nothing

like her own as he told the jarvey to drive on and shut the door.

'I have been away from London, otherwise I should have called on you.' The note in his answer was puzzling, an undercurrent of emotion she could not fathom. Wariness, perhaps, or even anger? Nothing quite made sense.

'I think your butler may be blackmailing me.'

'Milne?' The question was choked out.

'I have received two letters in the past week. One demanding one hundred pounds and the next five hundred. The first I paid, but the more recent one…' She stopped unable to go on and hating the way her voice shook.

'Where are they? The letters?'

'I burnt them both.'

'Unwise. Can you remember the exact words?'

She did, and parroting the messages made her feel slightly better. If he could help her, there might still be a way…

'How were the envelopes sealed?'

'With red wax.'

'And the slope to the writing?'

'Was unremarkable.'

'Did the footman remember anything of the way the second note had come?'

'I did ask. A child of the street brought that one, too.'

'The same child?'

Eleanor frowned. 'I did not bother him for a description.'

'Damn.'

'And the second drop?'

'Drop?'

'The place you were to leave the money?'

'He said I was to walk down Regent Street this morning and he would come and speak to me. But I did not go.'

The silence was thick and when he said no more she chanced her own observation. 'I didn't know who else to call on for help.'

He looked her straight in the eyes. 'You did not think that I could be the culprit?'

'No.'

When she smiled he swore. In French. She had never heard any of the words he used, but guessed them to be ripe given his tone of delivery. Even that made her feel better, for he was every bit as angry as she was.

'Did you tell your husband?'

She shook her head. 'He is ill and would not wish to know...'

'Then don't. I'll deal with it all, I promise you. If another letter comes, leave it sealed, but have it delivered straight to my town house.'

She nodded, the relief of having him shouldering the burden of her secret immense.

'Would they harm my daughter, do you think?'

'No.' He did not even hesitate, the certainty in his tone an elixir against all the 'what ifs' she had been imagining.

'I do not care about my reputation, but if Florencia is hurt because of this...'

'No one will harm her, I promise you, Eleanor. No one.'

'I will pay any expenses incurred, of course.'

He shook his head and placed one hand on his knee, palm up.

He would help her.

His eyes were black and undeniably furious. No milk-livered fop or dandy with little notion of the fighting arts, but a man who had survived the baser ways of others by his wits and by his knowledge. The scar across one whole side of his palm was a badge of experience.

A new worry surfaced. 'You would not kill anyone…?'

'…innocent?' He finished off the sentence and her disquiet heightened.

'England affords harsh punishments to those who take the law into their own hands.'

'You are the second person in the space of two weeks who has reminded me of the differences.'

'The second?'

'My brother Taris warned me off an affair of the heart.'

'Oh.' She coloured and looked out of the window. The dome of St Paul's could be seen far in the distance. Did he speak of a mistress perhaps, a kind of warning to make her realise the impossibility of anything intimate ever happening again between them?

Inside the carriage she could smell the soap he used, the perfume clean and unfussy. His hair caught all the colours of the light. Corn and wheat and pure plain silver. Cristo Wellingham was by far the most handsome man she had ever laid her eyes on and she could understand the fuss he had engendered in all the beating hearts of London's younger women. For a moment she wished she had been younger, prettier, unencumbered. And more daring. But she wasn't. She was a twenty-three-year-old married mother with the shame of sin about to be proclaimed to all who might listen.

Unless she could stop it!

'My husband is dying.' The words were out before she meant them to be and she blanched at the echo. She had not admitted that even to herself and to hear them said so unbidden was shocking. Still she could not take them back. 'I need him to go to the grave with a soul that is not troubled.'

'Is Florencia mine, Eleanor?' He asked the question a second time, and everything stopped. Breath. Blood. Movement.

They were no longer in a carriage on the road around London town, no longer part of a day scrawled with blue and green and yellow. Instead they sat in a void of empty loss, the grey whir of deceit pulling them apart, bruising his eyes and twisting his face into something that was not known.

'No,' she denied again, the word creeping between her lips, bending in question and in fright. One different word and a whole world could change with it. One other word and her daughter was no longer just hers. The regret that marked his face was only some comfort.

'I don't believe you. Martin was married twice before and there were no offspring from either marriage.'

'Both wives were barren.'

'Or perhaps you were already pregnant from our coupling and England had ceased to be an option to return to?'

Eleanor remembered the whispers about the Comte de Caviglione. A spy, the women had said in the Château Giraudon that night, and one of the cleverest around. She remained silent under the watchfulness of his gaze, the frown on his forehead deeper now as his glance fell to her hand wringing the fabric in her skirt this way and that. The cut-diamond face of her wedding ring sparkled like ice. Mocking everything.

'At Beaconsmeade you said that you loved me.'

The ache at the back of her throat almost made her cry out and say it again and again, here in the space of the carriage cocooned from society and propriety. Kiss me, she longed to demand, reach out and take away choice and kiss me, but he did not move, and the silence between them grew full with doubt and hesitancy.

Finally he spoke. 'I will station a man in your street, Eleanor, to watch for anyone who might contact you again.' All business and efficiency. She saw how he lifted his knees back so that even inadvertently he might not touch her.

'People will question...'

'This man will be like a breeze that fills only the cracks others miss.'

'A bit like you, then. A hidden man?'

He laughed, though she thought the sound forced.

'Is your mother still alive?'

She could never get used to the way he changed subjects. Almost on a whim.

'No. She died a few years before my grandfather did.'

'So when you came to Paris there was no one left?'

Hurt raced through her bones like the small flying insects that dissected the evenings at her childhood home. The last of the Bracewell-Lowens. Even years of time had not lessened the ache of it.

'There were never many of us in the first place…'

'Lord, Eleanor.' He held up his fingers as if to stop the words, stop the way she said them, fancy-free and offhand. 'You need someone…'

'I have Martin.'

'And when you don't?'

She pulled down the window and called to the driver to stop. When the carriage did so she unlatched the door and looked away.

'I shall never be a woman who would choose the wrong thing to do above the right one. Do you understand?' Steel coated her words. 'And in the light of that if you feel you can now no longer help me…'

He held up his hand and she faltered.

'"I wasted time and now doth time waste me."'

'From *Richard the Second*?'

'You know your quotes, my Eleanor, and I give you my word that from now on I shall not squander another second.'

'Eleanor, have you heard the news? Cristo Wellingham was involved in a fight near Blackfriars Bridge. It is said that he broke one man's nose and another man's arm. His family, as you can imagine, is not pleased.' Diana's face was full of distaste. 'A gentleman should not be seen in such circumstances and especially a lord freshly come from France and nearing the age of thirty.'

Sophie giggled. 'He is a very fine fighter from all the gossip I have been hearing…' She stopped as her mother frowned.

'Only reputation separates us from the *hoi polloi*, my girl, and things of this nature have the result of making those just beneath us in breeding sit up and ask questions. The Wellinghams have a duty to rein such wildness in.'

'Was he hurt?' Eleanor asked as soon as Diana stopped speaking.

'Several cuts around the eyes, apparently! The boy was always trouble, for goodness' sake, just look at that nasty business with your brother. In his favour I did hear that he went to Bornehaven Grange to try to explain what had happened with Nigel, but your uncle ran him off.'

Eleanor tried to imagine what the eighteen-year-old Cristo Wellingham might have said to her family. Nigel was dead by an accident at his hand according to the gossip and he had left England the following day, a son of Falder who was never to return to it. What forced a man to that kind of disconnection?

Another more worrying thought surfaced as well. What if the fight here in London had something to do with the blackmail letters that she had told him of? Would he be crucified by society for a promise he had made to her? A woman who would lie about the parentage of her own daughter?

Everything that had been simple was no longer, because, although another letter had not come, she found herself watching each and every stranger who came near to them. In the park. In the reading rooms at Hookham's. In the safety of shops she had once enjoyed wandering in.

Watching and fearing.

'I think we should have a walk after lunch for the day is lovely and I don't wish to miss it. Would you come too,

Eleanor? Martin is having a sleep after all and you have not been anywhere in days.'

Feeling the sun slanting into the room and Florencia tugging at her sleeve, Eleanor relented. With Diana, Sophie and Margaret and a multitude of other servants accompanying them, surely nothing could go wrong and Hyde Park on a Saturday was a busy and safe place.

Shaking away her nervousness, she took a breath. She wouldn't let the past trap her for ever and Cristo Wellingham had promised her that he would deal with any problems should they arise.

Still, to make certain that Florencia was safe, she would instruct her daughter to stay by her side.

An hour later Eleanor was becoming less and less sure of the wisdom of agreeing to such an outing as the clouds rolled in and the park emptied. Still, Diana seemed unperturbed by any oncoming weather.

'I tell you that it will not rain, Sophie, and a bit of wind and drizzle does wonders for any young girl's countenance. Keep up, Margaret, and you, too, Lainie. Florencia, hold your mother's hand as she has asked you to or I will instruct Molly to take you home immediately.'

Florencia conceded, even as Eleanor promised herself that this would indeed be the last walk she took with Martin's very bossy younger sister.

Already the first spits of rain worried her gown and she drew her daughter in closer.

'Up ahead there are some trees. We will shelter there until

Harold returns with the coach.' Even Diana had her limits of enduring a storm.

A line of oaks looked very isolated and forlorn in the wet. Still, she could do nothing except follow the group as they dashed towards them.

It was then that she saw them. Two men walking at an angle, cutting across the grass and looking straight at her. The tallest of them seemed vaguely familiar, though she could not for the life of her think how she could know him.

Grabbing Florencia's hand, she pulled her towards her family, shouting out for Diana to stop, but already the strangers were on her, the first one leaning down and calmly picking up her daughter. Florencia screamed even as Eleanor did not allow her fingers to break contact.

'I would advise you to let the girl go, *madame*. Any histrionics will make it difficult for both of you.'

In French!

The carousel of her mind spun backwards and stopped. This was the man who had burnt her thigh at the Château Giraudon with the red-hot tip of his smouldering cheroot. Shaking his words away, she reached for Florencia, fear making her movements heavy and slow.

'Let go of her, right now.' She could barely recognise the sound of her own voice.

But he did not listen, turning his back and taking the path away from the others. Hurrying to follow, she saw Diana behind them, shouting and gesturing. Too far away. Another man she had not seen suddenly reached out, his arm about her waist, lifting her off her feet as he jammed a heavy sack over her head. A sick plunge of nausea made her stomach lurch and she stumbled, the movement taking all breath from her body and making her see points of dancing black.

'Florencia.' The word hurt to say, but she tried again. A short curse in French stopped her as a hard object connected with her head. Then there was only darkness.

Chapter Thirteen

Cristo crouched against one of the piles under the warehouse, quiet against the river water. The sun slanted against the glass of a dirty window above him, smears of age and grease and dust. The only sunbeam for miles, he thought, his eyes scanning the alleyway winding up around the corner, the dark press of buildings sending shadowed danger into everything.

He was here because Etienne Beraud was in London. The Foreign Office had told him when Cristo had contacted them about the blackmail notes Eleanor had received, but he had disappeared, a known French spy who could only be up to no good.

Today, however, Cristo had intercepted a note with the name of his old rival upon it and written in a code that had been easily broken, a note that told of a safe house they were using by the docks.

Swearing softly, he rubbed at his left eye, aching from a punch he had failed to escape the evening before last when the piece of information had fallen into his hands.

Paris seemed to reach out and consume him again, the subterfuge of ten lonely years lying heavily across the last weeks in England when his body had begun to uncoil into something approaching a normal life. With a hat pulled down over his eyes he was the man he had once been, the knife strapped to his ankle sharp and honed and another one hidden beneath the folds of his shirt equally as keen. He made his breathing slower by sheer dint of will, a trick he had learned from endless nights of marking time.

Finally, just as the sun had gone and the moon had taken its place, there was movement and the sound of footsteps on the wooden decking.

Hoisting himself up, Cristo stayed under the shelter of shadow, a silent shape stalking his quarry without sound. When he was close enough he pulled the knife from his belt, the silver tang of it heavy in his hand as he pressed it against the throat of the one he had caught.

'*Pas un mot, vous comprendez?*'

Not a word, you understand?

As the man realized the danger, his fingers reached for his pocket. Cristo pressed his blade in harder and they instantly stilled.

'De Caviglione.'

'Dupont.'

Manners in the heart of death-dealing.

'Where is Beraud?'

'I do not know.'

The blade nicked through the cloth, drawing blood.

'Wrong answer. Where is he?'

True fear beaded Dupont's upper lip and the bottom one began to quiver.

'In the building with the tower next to this one! He has your lady.'

'He…? What…?' Anger made the words lethal and fear chilled Cristo to the bone. 'They have Eleanor? Why?'

The time to tread carefully was long gone and Dupont, reading his fury, began to sob. 'I did not know he planned to do this. The child is only young…'

A child as well? Florencia.

Lifting the heavy hilt of his knife, he brought it down hard across Dupont's temple and left him face down on the dirtied cobblestones.

Beraud's lair was exactly where Dupont had said it would be and Cristo came in through the back door, dispensing with the locks in less than a minute.

Two men outside the room on the second floor were on guard. He met them in French with his beret pulled down low.

'Beraud wants you downstairs now…'

By the time he had finished speaking they had seen his eyes and by then it was far too late. They fell quietly for large men and he dragged both into an empty room at one end of the corridor, binding their mouths, feet and hands with strips of leather he had brought with him for the purpose.

A chink of light showed beneath a door at the end of the passage way and even as he listened he heard the quiet crying of a child.

* * *

Eleanor came back to consciousness in a room that smelt of fish. Florencia was tucked in beside her, sobbing quietly. When Eleanor brought her finger to her mouth to ask for silence, she could hear the sea lapping at the floorboards.

A warehouse on the dock. She was sure that was where they had been taken and the next thought made her temples throb. If they were transported by boat out of London, any-thing might happen to them. Fear dried her mouth.

Lifting her other hand, she saw that the blood on her fin-gers was congealed and sticky. Pain lanced through her lip and her side and she shifted her position to accommodate the ache. To the left some twenty yards away the man from Paris and another stood talking, a pile of money stacked between them on a table.

Florencia shook in fear, hot tears running onto her silken dress and shadowing the yellow.

'It will be all right, Florencia. I promise.' Sometimes lies were a balm to truth but the terror in her was growing with each passing second.

'The man gave me a bon-bon.' She raised the sticky sweetness up, wailing as Eleanor knocked the treat from her hands and it rolled across the floor, collecting dust and wheat grains and fibre.

'You must not eat anything they give you,' she said even as she sidled to the right. There had to be something here she could hide, some solid sharp object that would allow her at least a moment of surprise. She found it in a hook embedded in a sack of grain, the shaft of it threaded with rope. When she tested the point, blood welled on the pad on her finger. If anyone touched Florencia, she would gouge out their eyes. She swore she would as she fitted the weapon into her palm.

Noises from outside made her start. A crash and some swearing and then the door was flung open, a voice she knew rising above others further out.

'Where is she?' The sound of a gun firing and then the stench of powder curling into the room!

Florencia screamed, frozen in terror, her dark eyes like two holes in her pale face, and then Cristo Wellingham was there, the boot of his heel through the door and the shot fired, loud and fierce, no quarter given. It was the metal shield he carried that had saved him, Eleanor realised later, though how he had known the man might aim for his head and not his chest…

Two knives flew almost in unison and then there was silence, the smoke curling as Cristo's eyes met her own, dark amber cold as steel.

'Eleanor?' Her name? She could see him say it, but there was no sound, only his mouth opening as the distance between them closed. Two feet and then one. Her face damp with blood and sweat and tears as she came against him, Florencia in her arms.

Her heartbeat was dull in her head and then they were outside in the rain, heavy and cleansing, the chill of it washing away all traces of death.

She grabbed at her daughter, hands threading through silver and silver, hardly knowing where one of them began and the other one ended. As sound returned his words were not in English but in French, quiet and honest and infinitely calming.

'It is over, Eleanor. You are safe.'

Nodding, she stayed there in his arms until her breathing softened. When she finally pulled away she saw his eyes were full of a pain that had nothing to do with the physical as he gazed at Florencia.

'You would not have told me?' His injured hand reached out for the silver in her hair.

Still in French. A protection, she realized, against his daughter listening. The muscles in his arms showed through the material in his jacket. Powerful. Strong. She watched as he touched Florencia for the very first time, infinite care and love in the movement.

'Tell me that you would have told me, damn it. Eleanor. I need to hear at least that.'

His eyes were closed now and the muscle on the side of the jaw rippled in tension.

'No. She is mine, Cristo, because to say anything else would be to destroy her. Don't you see that?'

The shadows in his eyes when he opened them again were bruised with both anger and want.

'Yet by saying nothing you destroy me?'

Her bottom lip quivered as the challenge registered. A choice, then? A man who had walked in the shadows of the world and whose sins were coming back to be visited upon those all about him, dangerous, perilous, the fortunate outcome of the evening's happenings only decided by a miracle! He had killed two men right in front of her eyes and never blinked once.

Pulling back, she broke contact, the guilt of another feeling sticking in her throat.

'The man you killed was from the Château Giraudon. I remember him as the one who hurt my thigh.'

He nodded. 'Etienne Beraud. He was a French spy.'

'As you were an English one? If anything had happened to Florencia because of our past…because of your past…'

Reality crashed in and his eyes acknowledged her withdrawal. Already the sounds of others were coming closer, the real world of London and its people, running steps and voices of authority. The constabulary. She saw the shape of their hats even as Cristo Wellingham drew away.

'Our coachman followed the carriage on foot to the docks after you were taken in the park, Lainie, and when he saw where they had stopped he came back to tell us.' Her sister-in-law's arms were firmly around her, helping her into the Dromorne conveyance, and settling a blanket across both her and Florencia's knees once inside. 'Martin was beside himself, of course, and had to be sedated, but I sent for the constabulary and we came straight here. I would not have believed it was Cristo Wellingham who took you until I saw him pulling at you, trying to make you stay. He will be hanged for this, of course.' Diana's voice was flat. 'He will be hanged and drawn and quartered for the kidnap of a lady and her child, and God knows what it will do to the Wellingham family name.' Barking out an order to the driver, she shut the door with a clang.

'No. It was not him…it was not Cristo Wellingham who did this. He saved us, Diana. He came and saved us.'

'Why?' Her sister-in-law's eyes had narrowed, the gleam in them deadened with the confession. 'Why would he do that, Eleanor? Why would a man with whom you have had very little contact risk his life to save yours?'

The truth was caught again in choice. Spare her reputation or save Cristo's life.

'I knew Cristo Wellingham intimately in Paris.'

Florencia between them looked up as the silence lengthened, and Eleanor saw the very second that the truth of her daughter's parentage dawned in Diana's glance.

'What have you done? Does my brother know any of this?' Her question was full of horror as she comprehended what it was that was implied. 'This sort of scandal will kill Martin and he has been nothing but kind to you. And my girls… This will ruin their chances of any union whatsoever if any of it gets out…you do know that?'

The weight of choice became heavier.

'If you could find it in yourself to protect our family and to say nothing…to let a man well connected take his chances…'

'There were people killed tonight, Diana. If he should be blamed for that, they would crucify him.' Eleanor shook her head firmly and reached for the handle of the carriage, but already the horses were moving at some speed. She felt a new dread creep into her heart as the anger flashed in her sister-in-law's eyes.

'Then you leave me no choice whatsoever, for both my brother and daughters and for Florencia. And for you, too, Eleanor! One day you might even thank me for saving you from yourself.'

'I don't understand.'

Banging twice on the roof of the carriage, Diana looked at her sadly.

'Unfortunately, my dear, you soon will.'

Cristo was thrown into goal, the baton marks on his shoulders protesting the movement. His legs were shackled and one of his eyes was swollen closed. The constabulary had come into the chaos and found him guilty, the blood on his clothes, the hysteria of Eleanor's sister-in-law, the gathering group of onlookers who had all pointed him out as one of the French kidnappers.

The blood on his hands had convicted him, the garb he had donned for his sojourn in the heart of the docks doing the rest. No longer an English gentleman. Only a felon with scant regard for the letter of the law.

No light punishment. No careful handling. For six hours now he had been kicked and punched and hurt, and still Eleanor did not come.

Could not come, Cristo reasoned, the truth of all that had happened closing in on him. Could not come because to do so would ruin her reputation completely. It was only that thought that kept him silent. Only the thought of protecting what was left of her honour.

But for how long? The thought of Ashe and Taris worried him. When would they know of the night's happenings?

Sitting on the cold stone floor, he nursed his right hand. Two fingers broken and his thumbnail gone; the jagged remains of what was left hurt like hell and he tore the final piece off with his teeth before sucking at the blood that welled.

His shirt was lost, too, and his shoes and the watch that his mother had given him when he was eleven. All around him the groans and shouts of other prisoners echoed, a reminder of other times when he had been bound and hurt and held.

But here in England it was different. His eyes skimmed the locks on the door. Two minutes and he would have them opened. Another five and he would be in fresh air. The fastening on his legs was such child's play he might have released the chains in his sleep.

'Ye'll be wanting a drink, no doubt.' The voice of the guard broke into his thoughts as a stream of water was thrown through the bars. The cold made him start even as training held him still.

'Thank you.'

The curse was ripe and the cup hit him fully on the cheek, breaking open the skin. 'With a noose around that pretty neck, ye may not be as polite.'

He refrained from answering and when the footsteps receded he stood, a dizzy lightness of head making him reach for the wall behind.

'Steady,' he said to himself and sucked at the moisture covering his arms. Even a little liquid was better than none at all and he needed his wits fully about him.

Florencia.

A daughter.

Their daughter.

Almost five. The same age as William and Alfred, Taris and Beatrice's twins.

Part of a family. A big family. A child of Falder and of the Carisbrook line and the de Caviglione blood that he had inherited from his mother.

God! He had seen himself in her chocolate eyes and silvered hair, reflections of his own childhood in the determined set of her jaw and the sweep of her forehead.

Eleanor had been eighteen and pregnant when she had simply stepped out of his carriage into a European winter. How could that have felt, hemmed in as she was by ruin and by the mistake of identity shattering every single tenet of proper behaviour and righteous convention that she had no doubt been raised to believe in.

Slapping his hands against the stone, he pushed away from the wall. No matter what happened now he would protect her. Protect them. This was his responsibility. He would say nothing of the threat of kidnap or of the identity of Beraud and his henchmen until he knew exactly what it was that Eleanor wanted to be said.

She lay drifting between night and day, reaching for the sweet smell of something close.

'Drink up, Lainie dear. It will help you.' A feminine voice that she knew well. Diana? Leaning forwards, she did as she was told and the room swam into bands of colour. Pink and red and orange.

She laughed as the hues mixed together and the thoughts in her head that were difficult glided away on the edge of peace.

'Florencia?' A name that was important. She reached for the sound of it even as the mist rose up again, the close timbre of the voice receding into distance.

Chapter Fourteen

'You killed these criminals in defence of a woman and her child, Cris. Tell the law of your relationship with Eleanor Westbury and the letters that were sent to her demanding money and that will be the end of it. They will believe you for who you are, and you can come home.'

Asher was there again. Had he been there already today? The minutes had turned into hours and then into more, as one day moved into two. Time skewered and bent into a never-ending stretch, the cold water, the careful bruising, shivering in black nights on a hard cobbled floor.

He had clothes now and food and while his brothers were about nothing untoward ever happened. He made it his mission in life not to complain about ill treatment and to never question the whereabouts of Eleanor Westbury.

Still, today Ashe had come armed with news. The Dromorne family had decamped into the country, to heal, it was rumoured, and to forget. One of their maids had let it slip to Beatrice's servant. Eleanor had left before the others with her daughter and sister-in-law, her things packed up in her absence.

To forget.

About him.

Her choice had been made in the aftermath of the fury and he could do nothing save stand by it. He had seen the anger in her eyes and understood exactly what had brought it there.

The silver strands of his daughter's hair flew like a flag of virtue in his face.

'I could break you out.' Ashe's voice was low-whispered, the knife he carried slipped into the straw on the edge of Cristo's cell.

'I could do that for myself, Brother.'

'Then what stops you?'

He only smiled.

'I will ride north with the Wellingham lawyers and demand Eleanor and Martin Westbury tell the truth.'

'And I will deny everything. Eleanor and Florencia stay safe. No scandal. No muck-raking. No gossipy outrage outlining the stigma of her birth and of my part in it.'

'And what of you in here? How long do you think you can last?' Ashe turned and drove his fist into the stone. 'Hell, Cris, you're more stubborn than Taris ever was, even at his worst of times, and that's saying something. Besides, if Lady Dromorne does not even have the courage to confess to the whole fiasco I'd say she wasn't worth the life you seem to want to throw away so carelessly.'

Cristo turned from his brother's words, the truth in them undeniable.

Eleanor had not come.

She had not even sent a missive to see that he still lived. For all that she might know he could be dangling now on the end of a rope, hanged for a crime that was not his. But even that thought was not quite correct. The crime had been his five years ago when he had taken her for a whore at the Château Giraudon and used her in a way no gentleman should ever use a lady. This was his penance. His punishment. The completion of a debt.

'So you would sacrifice the Wellingham name for the Dromorne one?' Asher again, his voice still lowered.

Anger forced his first real emotion. 'I have sacrificed much in the name of others, brother. This one is entirely for myself.'

'Guilt is a hard taskmaster.'

The pale eyes of Eleanor raised in supplication from a velvet bed shimmered before him, the wintertime Paris such a long way from a London gaol.

'No, Asher. It is only easy.'

'I cannot make him see sense, damn it, and Eleanor Westbury accepts all correspondence and returns none of her own.'

'Yet if we give the truth of the matter to the law he will never forgive us.' Taris finished the last of his brandy and poured himself another one.

Bea and Emerald sat with them in the downstairs library of the Carisbrook town house, all their children sent off with their nannies and myriad servants to Falder.

'Azziz and Toro could get him out.' Emerald bit at her fingernails as she said it. 'They could bring him home.'

'This is London, Emmie, not Jamaica, and a thousand constables would be after our heads should we be implicated. Besides, Cris would hate us for it.'

Beatrice walked to the window. 'If Martin Westbury dies soon, Cristo might achieve exactly what he wants. A widow of spotless reputation and a child who is for ever seen as the offspring of her husband.'

'And what if he lasts for years, Bea? What of the charges that Cristo faces right now?' Taris's voice was strained. 'How can we get him out of there and have the charges gone without needing the help of the Dromornes?'

A knock at the door made them all start, and the butler came in with a sheath of paper sealed in red wax and ribboned. It was addressed to the Duke of Carisbrook. Ashe took it quickly and began to read.

'The suit against Cristo is to be dropped.'

Taris shook his head. 'Who talked, Ashe?'

'Martin Westbury. It is stated here that there had been notes sent that had intimated kidnap. Dromorne also said that he had paid Cristo a substantial sum of money to protect his wife from harm given his own ill health, and that all the subsequent mayhem resulted from that bargain.'

'Let's hope the fact that he was the only Westbury willing to do anything to save Cristo's skin might make our brother think twice about his apparent fascination for the fickle-hearted Lady Dromorne.'

Beatrice stood and joined her husband. 'I cannot believe that she would simply let Cristo hang for an offence that she knew was not his. There must be something we do not know about in all of this…'

Taris held up his hand. 'Right now it's our brother I am more concerned about, Bea.' He lifted his watch from his pocket and felt for the time. 'Ten o'clock. Could we get him out tonight?'

'Damned if they can try to stop us,' Ashe answered as he called for the carriage.

The mist seemed to be clearing, widening, the sweet taste of freedom further away now and pain all that was left of any of it.

She was sick into the bowl held beneath her face, many times, sweat moistening her skin and making her clammy.

'There, there, Lainie. You will be all right now. It is over. You are safe.'

Martin's voice. The quiet tones comforting. She held on to the hand he offered. Her lips were dry and the skin in her throat was parched.

'Water?' A glass was brought to her lips as he tipped her head to taste it and more clouds cleared.

'And your sister?'

'Has gone. I sent her back to Scotland when I realised what was happening. Her husband has promised she will not venture into England again for many years.'

'Cristo Wellingham?'

'Is safe. I made sure of it.'

'And Florencia?'

'Is at this moment doing her lessons in the schoolroom with her governess.'

When he raised her hand to his lips to kiss it, she saw she was only skin and bone. 'How long have I been like this?'

'Two weeks.'

The time had her gulping back fear. 'Fourteen whole days? What happened after…London?'

'Diane took you north to an inn and administered laudanum. The doses were so high it took us some time to wean you off it.'

'Us?'

'The Dromorne doctor is in attendance.'

Eleanor lay her head back on the pillow and tried to take stock of everything. Where was Cristo Wellingham now? She had no way of asking, however, for already she could see in her husband's eyes a disappointment that laid every other truth bare.

'I did not lie to you, Martin, about Florencia. I just did not tell you the name of her father.'

He smiled at that. 'And if I had asked, would you have told me?'

She considered this. 'You never did ask.'

Closing her eyes, she felt tears leak between her lids, the tight ache in her throat making talking harder.

'Nevertheless, I would have appreciated honesty that night you saw Wellingham again at the theatre. Surely then, Eleanor, you might have said something?'

The gap she had always felt between them widened, lies stretching out what little that had held them together. With only a push everything might break and the circles of tiredness beneath his eyes were dark, worry and illness mixed into deep bruises on his skin.

A man caught between the truth of expedience and struggling to do the right thing. His sister's betrayal, his wife's shame and his own body's failings. An honourable man who deserved a lot more than the hand he had been dealt. She reached out.

'I am so very sorry.'

One finger came across the line of her cheek, wiping away the tears, soft as kindness. 'I should not wish for our name to be bandied about in the way that any confession could easily let it.'

'And neither should I.'

'Cristo Wellingham has said nothing at all. To anyone. He holds his tongue for the sake of our daughter.'

This time Eleanor could not even answer, the lump in her throat growing, and she had no idea of what might happen next. Cristo had his own family to consider and he was not a man who courted publicity, but in saying nothing he had in effect let her go. Lord, what must he think of her, then? A woman of so little moral fibre that she could not even rouse herself to write a thank-you note?

'Did you tell him about Diana…about the laudanum?'

'Yes, and he has given me his guarantee of confidence on the matter.' There was a tone in her husband's voice that she had never heard there before and Eleanor guessed it to be the grief of losing respect for a favoured sister. She swallowed. At least Cristo Wellingham knew why she had not been able to come to London and exonerate him. She did not dare to voice her relief, however, as her husband began to talk again.

'I have rented a town house in Bath and we shall repair

there immediately. The waters warrant much in the way of a cure and my cough has worsened…'

She smiled through her tears. 'Florencia would like that.'

'Wellingham has promised he will never set foot in the city so long as we are there. He sends you only his very best wishes for the future.'

'You have seen him?'

'A number of times, my dear, and his brothers stood with him on each occasion. Family solidarity is an undervalued commodity to my mind, and the sense of protecting reputation is well understood by every old lineage. He wants his name unsullied.'

Eleanor swallowed, imagining the conversation. Unsullied. For the best. For protection. For Florencia. Bleakness covered all emotion and what had budded began again to wilt, blighted before it had even had time to flourish.

'Bath will be lovely at this time of year,' she said, and felt the weight of motherhood hard upon her shoulders even as she wiped away her tears.

Cristo remodelled Graveson Manor using all of the taste he had acquired from years of living in Paris. Simple. Expensive. Chic. He oversaw the laying of the marble floor in the portico entrance and the coloured glass in the atrium that joined the old wing to the new one. No detail was too small to find unimportant. The library, the music room, the ballroom that Beatrice had insisted he include, even the nurseries that graced the third floor of the structure, painted in lemon and green.

He never walked there again after finishing those particular chambers, because he knew that without Eleanor there would not be infants.

One suite on the end of the corridor, however, he did often visit. This room was fashioned in pink and silver, a trail of stuffed animals on numerous shelves waiting for the one little girl in the world who would never play with them.

Florencia. Her name was engraved in his heart like a tattoo, ineradicable and permanent, and the reason for every single thing that he did.

His own room he left plain and barely touched. A single bed, an armoire and a wardrobe. No mirror to fashion his likeness as he prepared for sleep, and no space for another body. Only necessity graced this chamber. A brush. A block of soap next to a pitcher. A bottle of fine French brandy for the nights when sleep would not arrive and the morning seemed a long way off.

Martin Westbury had been most civil when he had come to call on him in London. He had thanked Cristo for the help rendered to his wife and then he had taken breath through the difficulty of a disease that had much worsened and asked for a moment in private.

His brothers had left him to wait outside and as the door closed the mask of the man before him had fallen into grief. A broken man and all at his account!

'My wife, Eleanor, is a good woman and a brave one. I would like you to know at least that.'

He nodded more out of expectation than of any real feeling because she had neither come nor written and almost two weeks had gone by with every single moment counted.

'She has told me of your…connection.' Dromorne held up his hand as Cristo went to speak. 'I have the energy to say what I want to only once.' He waited as Cristo nodded and settled back.

'All I have in the way of possessions, save the entailed buildings and title, will go directly to Eleanor and Florencia and I am a very rich man. But money cannot buy back reputations and at the moment theirs are lying in the balance. Were you to talk, I doubt that even I would have the wherewithal to save them.' Another tear traced its way across his cheeks, falling on one armrest of his wheelchair and sliding onto legs marked by thinness.

'You did not disclose your association with my wife in gaol under severe provocation and you did not gossip on your release. I respected that. Eleanor, however, has decided that you are too dangerous to ever be allowed near our daughter again. It is the problem of your past, you understand, and your questionable connections. She has asked me to come to tell you that she will allow nothing to compromise Florencia.'

Silence counted down the moments.

'So you wish for me to leave England?'

'No. I have arranged a place for my family in Bath. It shall be that city that is off limits to you if Florencia's chance of a future is to be secured. I have spoken to Eleanor about this and she has agreed. It was a foolish and ill-thought out flight of fancy for her to have agreed to see you again and one that cannot be repeated. My wife is most explicit on that point.'

'I see.' Cristo balled his fists and laid them at his side.

He wished the man might just leave with his promises and illness and inherent logic. Eleanor and Florencia were lost to him through the strict rules of propriety and respectability every bit as much as they were through sheer and utter cowardice.

'If I were younger, I might call you out for this, Wellingham.'

Cristo held his glance, the fury inside him lending any civility a brittle air. 'Perhaps such a duel might work to my advantage, my lord.'

Dromorne smiled at the insult and refused to be drawn into the argument further, rapping his cane heavily on the floor. The door opened and he was gone, only the sound of his wheels against the highly polished parquet as they receded into the distance. Asher and Taris came in to stand beside him.

'It is settled,' he said, hoping that the catch in his voice was not a permanent disability, as the blood in his heart emptied into ice. Betrayal melded seamlessly with disbelief.

'Did you tell him your side of the story?'

Cristo nodded at Asher's question, knowing full well that he had not, but the wish for his siblings to think kindly of Eleanor Westbury made him lie as he spoke again.

'Eleanor sends me her best wishes and her sincere thanks, but she has a daughter to protect.'

Taris's curse had been ripe.

Turning to the window, Cristo was glad for the space and for the first time since he had left Paris he missed his old life in the Château Giraudon, missed its danger and its clarity, the sides of wrong and right so easily defined. Here he felt he had wandered into a land of choices or a hall of mirrors, every direction cursed by circumstance and conduct.

Eleanor was married and she was a loyal wife. Nothing could change that save the death of Dromorne. She was also a mother who loved her daughter.

A tumbler of brandy came from nowhere and he swallowed the lot, liking the way it coated anger with its own particular brand of acceptance.

Martin Westbury had spent the following hours in St Paul's Cathedral having a dialogue with his maker.

'I lied to protect us all, Lord.' He thought of his sister and her ill-guided actions and how she had been bundled back to Edinburgh where her husband's family held a seat.

He thought of his parents and his ancestors and the goodness that had always imbued the Dromorne name since time immemorial. He thought of Florencia and her silver hair and eyes that were exactly those of Cristo Wellingham and for the first time in his life he swore in a house of God because he knew that Eleanor Bracewell-Lowen had never truly been his.

A wife in name only. A woman he had never touched. Her illness had precluded it at first and in the later years his infirmity had robbed him of any feeling in that region of his being.

But he could change. They could change, and, if God could give him the chance of a second destiny, then who would know what might follow? He smiled, making the sign of the cross above his heart in respect to a wiser deity who had given him direction. Tonight he would show Eleanor that he had forgiven her lies by coming to her room and allowing her the opportunity of sexual expression that a twenty-three-year-old must crave.

It was, after all, the very least that he could do.

Chapter Fifteen

Eleanor went to bed early and left the curtains wide, wide open, so that the moon shone on the bed and lightened her room with silver. The colour of Cristo Wellingham's hair. She stroked the beam on her sheets with her little finger so that the shadow did not blot out the light and whispered his name against the silence.

Martin had arrived home late and she had smelt strong liquor on his breath, but even that had not been the most unusual thing that had happened this evening. When she had spoken her goodnight he had beckoned her down to him and taken her face in his hands, looking at her in a way she had not seen him do before. Almost sensual! Distaste surfaced, followed by a bolt of fear. Did he think she would want that from him now? Did he imagine the knowledge of her transgressions allowed him a right he had not as before taken?

She sat up, lighting the candle and watching the wick take to flicker yellow into all the shadowy corners. Outside she heard her husband's chair whirring by just as it did every evening.

But tonight it stopped.

Her breath froze in her throat as the handle began to turn and the door was pushed inwards. Slowly, as if he should not wish to wake her should she be asleep. She cursed the flame at her side, but it was too late to blow it out; when his face came around the portal she made herself smile.

'Martin?' She hoped there was just enough question in it to be short of rudeness.

'Eleanor. I am glad you are still awake.'

The door closed behind him and her heartbeat quickened.

'You wish to talk?' she said and drew the blanket up.

He stopped next to her and reached across for one hand, taking it into his own in the way of a husband who did not suppose anything other than acquiescence.

'I spent a number of hours at St Paul's Cathedral today, my dear, asking the Lord for a way forwards from all of this.'

'I see.' His thumb nudged the material on her sleeve aside so that her neck was exposed and before she could stop him his hand dug into the silk in her bodice, her left breast fitting into coldness. Only shocking.

'I think the lack of any physical contact between us should be at an end, my love.'

'You do?' She tried to pull away, but his grip tightened.

'We are husband and wife, although consummation for me is somewhat of a problem, there are things that I am still able to manage that could bring you pleasure.'

He rolled the material back and let go of her breast, exposing the ample flesh to his glance and to the light before he bent down. Suckling, like a child, the bald spot in the back of his head easily visible.

Her husband. His right. Her duty. She sat as still as she could whilst moonlight faded into cloud. When he had finished she tried to smile at him, glancing down again as he repositioned the fabric in her nightgown and placed the sheet back.

'It is a beginning, Lainie, and a good one. I shall worship your body as a shrine and hope with all that I am able that my ministrations bring you some portion of pleasure and some allotment of ease.'

Nodding, she watched as he departed, the door shutting behind him and the quiet settling yet again.

A shrine. A duty. Pleasure? Ease? One hand went to her mouth to stop the aching sobs she knew would come, whilst the other gathered the fabric on her breast and wiped the wetness dry.

Nowhere to go and no one to help her. Shocked, she turned into the down of her pillow and cried until sleep overtook her, and in her dreams there was a different man whose lips wove all the magic that her husband's had failed to do.

Martin met her in the blue parlour the next morning with a particular smile and a wink. Today he looked healthier than he had in a long while, and another layer of guilt was added to those already present. Florencia sat between them, chatting about a puppy she had seen in the park and about a drawing she had completed of him on her return home.

'He was black and white, Mama, with long ears. When he walked he wobbled and Miss Walsh bade me not to laugh too loud. When will Aunty Diana be back, Mama? I want to tell her about him.'

'She has much to do in Scotland, Florencia. I doubt that she will be back for a while.' Martin's voice held a note of censure she hoped her daughter would not notice.

'But Margaret and Sophie are missing out on the balls. Some of their dresses are still in the cupboards.'

'We will send them on, Florencia.' Eleanor placed her daughter's napkin so that the crumbs of the cake a maid had brought in did not stain her skirt. She did not even bother to unravel her own because she felt no hunger whatsoever.

Ten hours before she would retire again for the evening. Ten hours before the next 'pleasure and ease' might begin yet again. The clock ticked on at an alarming speed and the spots of age on the back of her husband's hands were plainly visible in the light. The vision of slender fingers wreathed in gold replaced it.

The pile of cards on the sideboard suddenly offered a sanctuary.

'The Benetts have asked us to a dinner party this evening, and were most hopeful that we should be able to come.'

Martin took a sip of tea. 'If you should like to go…'

'I should.' The words sounded desperate even to her ears.

'Then perhaps we could manage it for a little while.'

Florencia clapped her hands and looked up, her eyes as wide as saucers. 'What shall you wear, Mama?'

'You might like to help me choose, my darling,' Her daughter's returned smile made the day bearable again.

'It seems the Dromornes are often out and about in Bath, Cristo. They were more circumspect here from what I remember, though the husband's ailment appears much recovered.'

Jack Henshaw, Asher's oldest friend, placed *The Times* down on the mahogany table and downed the last of the brandy in his glass. 'She is cutting quite a figure in the city, according to the article. An Original, the writer supposes, and all the women copying her style.' He frowned as memory was sifted. 'I recall her being quite staid in her taste. A young woman dressed as a rather older one, do you not agree?'

Cristo shook his head and declared no opinion whatsoever, but sat perfectly still as Jack droned on.

'It says that Lady Dromorne rarely misses the chance to socialise and that she has begun to take up the habit of leaving every party awfully late.'

'And her husband?'

'Is home in bed waiting, perhaps. A man of singular trust and devotion, poor fool him.'

'You are implying her to be loose?'

Jack smiled and his eyes met Cristo's through the glasses he had begun to wear whilst reading.

'Your tone is more than impartial, Cris.'

'And your hearing is as poor as your eyesight, Jack.'

'Eleanor Westbury is described as the most beautiful woman to ever grace Bath.' Again his brow crinkled. 'Perhaps the air there suits her constitution well. It has been a good while, after all, since they departed this place and settled in the country.'

Nine months, two weeks and three days, Cristo thought, and hated himself for the counting, though the appearance of Taris and Asher at the club allowed the subject of the Dromornes to at least be dropped.

Or so he had thought until Asher raised their name again.

'There has been an accident, Cris. In Bath.'

His heart stopped. He swore it did and swore, too, that all the blood from his face drained into pale.

'Eleanor or Florencia?' He could not be careful with their names, not when they could already be lost to him.

'Martin Westbury. He was hit by a carriage as he crossed the street in his chair yesterday. He was killed instantly.'

'Lord.' Jack gestured to the waiter to bring a bottle and more glasses. 'So the illness that he suffered from for all those years didn't kill him after all? What irony is there in that?'

Taris answered directly. 'The chance of a quick death as opposed to a lingering one. I think he could count himself fortunate.'

'Was anyone else hurt?' Cristo had found his voice again.

'No. It seems his servant jumped well out of the way.'

'A loyal subject.' Jack laughed, though Taris was not quite finished speaking.

'Would it be wise to go and give our condolences, do

you think? The Dromorne family is repairing back here to London as we speak.'

'Why the hell would we want to do that, Taris? The woman almost killed Cristo.' Asher's question was harsh, his expression puzzled.

'Beatrice felt it the right thing to do when she heard the news. She said Cris would probably feel the same.'

'Yes. I'd like to go.' Cristo was infinitely grateful for the suggestion.

'Then we will go together.' Ashe laid his hand on his shoulder. Martin Westbury was dead and Eleanor was alone and yet all Cristo could feel was numbness.

Eleanor had dressed Florencia in her black dress and tied the ribbon at her waist, placing the satin so that it hung in two long strips down to the hem. Her own gown held not a hint of any colour save for darkness, the black bombazine wrapped around her figure in the most sombre of shades.

Dead. Martin. Not of illness or of lack of breath, but of an accident. She wished she could have had one chance to say goodbye. Another thought, however, lurked in the background of the more charitable ones.

Relief.

Pushing the word down, she turned to the bishop who had come to the house to give his sincere condolences on the loss of her spouse. He also assured her that a marriage of tenderness and love in this earthly realm, such as theirs had indeed been, would one day be repeated in the celestial one if only she was patient.

'I will certainly remember the thought, Bishop Pilkington,'

she returned and dabbed at her eyes with a handkerchief, her tears those for the man who had found her in the chapel alone in Aix-en-Provence and taken her and her newly born daughter to Florence. With love.

'There have been a great many people who have come to pay your husband their last respects over the past few days.'

Eleanor nodded, Martin's standing in the community of the *ton* had always been substantial and his wealth cemented his position.

'I noticed the Carisbrook conveyances pulling up as I arrived here.'

Eleanor dropped the Bible she held and it fell to the ground with a loud bang. When she made no move to bend and pick it up a maidservant hovering in the shadows bobbed down to retrieve it.

'Thank you.' The tremble in her voice was obvious and the bishop reached out for her hand and held it within his own.

'God sends us these trials in life, my dear, but he also sends us the wherewithal to rise above them and create a new journey.'

The Carisbrook conveyances? Cristo Wellingham. Had he married? Had he come to mock her? Had he brought his family to demand the return of her daughter now that her husband was gone?

Another thought also struck her and she unfastened the piece of black silk around her neck, bending to her daughter and winding the fabric around her hair to hide the silver.

'It is good manners to cover our hair when we have lost somebody very dear,' she explained as Florencia reached up to see just what her mother had fashioned.

'Like your one, Mama?'

The veil was pulled down and the lace let through only imprints of what was beside her. Still, with a thick barrier between herself and the man who had never contacted her again, she allowed herself to be lead from the small parlour out into the larger one across the hall, her daughter's hand firmly kept within her own.

Cristo looked up and Eleanor was there, a veil pulled across her face, hiding everything. Florencia stood next to her, black silk strangely placed around her head, small sprigs of silver escaping the concoction. She looked taller than when he had last seen her, a gold chain with a locket at her neck lending her the air of an older girl.

Eleanor Westbury, on the other hand, had lost weight and a waist that had always been small was now worryingly thin. The chestnut of her hair beneath the veil was highlighted by the darkness of her clothes.

Beatrice next to him laid her hand across his arm, just for a moment, and Emerald on her other side caught his eyes, the turquoise in them, as she observed Florencia, holding an unnerving knowledge.

He looked away. The room was dressed with white lilies and new spring roses. A family banner in purple wool was draped over a large portrait of the Earl of Dromorne set up on a plinth by the window.

Cristo imagined the soul of Westbury castigating him from Heaven, a ghoulish form of sullen morality.

Distance, it might say, and the keeping of a promise, the spectre questioning his very right to be in the house.

Reaching down for the headrest of the sofa in front of him, he held on as if it were a lifeline in a rapidly sinking ship.

A man of the church he recognised as Bishop Pilkington was making much of his departure, his monologue a solemn and depressing piece reminding those in the room of the impermanence of life and of the coming of death.

'Everyone here will die,' he began and caught Cristo's eye with an added fervour. 'Every single one of us here will die just as this man has and be welcomed into the kingdom of our Lord.'

Now Cristo knew why he seldom ventured into a religious institution or sought out the company of those within it. He coughed to clear his throat and Eleanor turned, her head angled. Listening. He saw the shape of her right ear adorned with a single perfect pearl. Lust shot through his body like a spear, unexpectedly brutal.

Shifting, he caught Asher's eye and looked away just as quickly, the tenure of his breath shaky. Reciting the conjugations of verbs in Latin helped to calm him. His mind ran across sequences determining pattern as his daughter shifted in her seat, one hand reaching for an itch on her neck. He watched her fingers and her nails and a bruise that sat at the base of her thumb. A small injury. Another moment lost to him. He wished he might have reached forwards and touched her, held his hand across her own and felt her warmth.

But of course he could do nothing of the sort. He was a stranger and a man whom she had seen only once in the heart of chaos. He dropped his gaze as she looked at him and sat perfectly still.

'Stop fiddling, Florencia.' Eleanor whispered the words and felt Cristo Wellingham there like an ache that had no ending. Just to the left of her. Five feet away. If she closed her eyes she might smell him, the scent of man and strength and warmness. She hoped he did not see the racing pulse in her throat or the tremor in her jaw. Her eyes rested on Martin's portrait and on the flowers and the crest and the small likeness of Heaven that her daughter had placed there on the plinth. Hidden beneath the lilies. A drawing of the sun and puppies and all the bon-bons in the world. Given that Martin had hated animals and anything very sweet, that left only the sun to see him on his way.

The Dromorne villa in Florence had been drowned in summer when she had arrived there, grey with fatigue and heartsick. Her tiny son had gone and Italy was a place too far for his soul to find her, but she remembered the warmth as she had stepped from the carriage into the light. She had done little else that long and hot summer save sleep and eat.

The Bishop at her side spoke again of the circle of life and the acceptance of death and the solace that one could find in the eternal love of God. In the rush of memory the reality of it all became focused and Eleanor felt the tears well behind her eyes for a husband who had been a good man and a friend.

* * *

She was crying. Cristo could see the tears mopped up by a kerchief that looked suspiciously masculine. He saw the way her hands shook and saw the tremors in her throat as she swallowed back grief and tried to find strength.

Asher was speaking now as the Carisbrook representative and Cristo simply listened. The sun slanted in through the window, covering everything with a strange light, and the Bishop, noticing it, relegated such a shimmer to the way of our Lord and the golden glow of redemption.

A letter of sorts stuck out on one corner of a substantial array of flowers and Cristo determined the end of a rainbow drawn across it.

Florencia's handiwork, perhaps? He wished that he might have seen more of the final goodbye to the only father she had ever known; as Eleanor stood, their eyes caught, hers plainly visible through a lacy veil.

Shock and want spread across something he could only explain as utter helplessness and his fists clenched at the material in his jacket so that he would not reach out. His breath shook with relief as she turned.

Florencia's dark eyes were staring at the floor and for that at least he was glad. On her feet she wore little black boots with three buttons on each side of the opening. The right one was scuffed at the toes.

And then it was time to go, time to step forwards and offer individual sympathies. Cristo was pleased Bea and Taris went before him with Ashe and Emerald behind, for sandwiched between Wellinghams he felt a little less visible. The day outside through the glass at the window was cold but blue. The leaves on the trees that lined the driveway were beginning to bud, light green against the limbs of winter.

He would come to give his condolences and she would have to touch him. He would come with his public face and his private thoughts, a man with a lot of reasons to keep the distance he so obviously sought.

Did his promise to stay away from her still exist now that Martin was gone? With Florencia's name secured for eternity would he wish for any more contact between them?

Another more worrying thought also occurred. Would Florencia recognise him as the one who had come into the warehouse to save them?

Beatrice-Maude came first and Eleanor felt indifference in the way she clasped her hands.

'I am sorry for your loss, Lady Dromorne.' Only that. She passed by as quickly as was considered proper and her husband lingered for a second or so longer. Then Cristo was there, his hand held awkwardly.

'Please accept my condolences.'

Her fingertips rested in his, the gloves they both wore a barrier to everything. He had not so much as raised his eyes to see her, his hair the colour of a spider web in the light.

Just this second.

Just this chance.

Her fingers clamped over his in a motion all of their own, desperate, reckless, melded into a knowledge that should she not try here, she might lose him for ever.

'Please…?'

She could not say more for her throat had closed up into

thickness and the words just would not come. Beside her one of Martin's cousins coughed.

Releasing his hand, she felt him slip away, from her, the side of his face and then the back of his head, his gloved hand reaching out to the next person in the line and the same words upon his tongue.

'Please accept my condolences.'

The air was so thin she could barely find breath, only him, here and then gone, only his touch through two layers of fabric and every single part of her longing for more.

Her fingers burned anger into his soul. More than nine months had passed since they had last seen each other and the time for an apology for her lack of contact was far and away over.

Even a letter might have sufficed.

He pushed the thought aside and concentrated on other things. The gilded carved cornices in the ceilings and the tall windows with their elaborate heavy curtains.

'We need not stay longer.' Asher turned to him, concern and worry written on his face, though Emerald had hung back and was now speaking with Eleanor.

'I should not wish to listen to the Bishop Pilkington every Sunday,' Beatrice said as they reached the carriage and Taris laughed.

'Fundamentalism has a form of judgement, Bea, that is often fashioned in a wavering zeal. He sounded young. Young enough to be saved by his vacillating faith, would you say?'

'Hell would have to freeze over first,' Ashe cut in, 'and I for one can't wait for a drink.'

Eleanor saw that the Wellinghams were laughing, their happiness in her unending sorrow almost a sacrilege.

'A very dear friend of mine has a house in High Wycombe that you would be most welcome to use. It is small, you understand, but very beautiful. A sanctuary, if you like.' Emerald Wellingham held her hand in a way that was endearing.

'Thank you for the kind offer, but—'

'Being alone in the city, Lady Dromorne, is very different to being alone in the country. Just remember that. Besides, no one would question your business there. I would make very sure of it.' Turquoise eyes bore into hers and Eleanor got the impression she was trying to say something completely different. 'If you should change your mind, I would be happy to hear from you and remember that things are not always exactly as they seem.'

Eleanor could not quite determine the Duchess of Carisbrook's motive in the warning. All the rest of the family had passed her by with only the most cursory of greetings, but this woman was almost ardent in her advice. Disengaging her hand, she stepped back.

'I thank you again, your Grace.'

'Emmie. It is how my friends call me.'

Eleanor stayed silent.

'My son Ashton is just a little older than your daughter and we have puppies at the town house at the moment. Perhaps your little girl might like to come and play with them?'

Eleanor smiled. It was hard to remain distant under such an onslaught of friendliness.

'Puppies?' Florencia pushed herself forwards. 'I love puppies.'

'Do you indeed, my dear? Then it is settled. Your mother must bring you to visit before they grow too large and you miss them altogether.'

'Can we, Mama? Please can we?'

In the face of all the sadness and tears Eleanor found herself nodding her head and arranging a date and time for the following week. Even though they were in mourning it would be a quick and private visit and it would be nice to see laughter again on her daughter's face.

Chapter Sixteen

Dressed in unending black, Eleanor exited the conveyance that had been sent by Emerald Wellingham to pick them up. The previous week had been difficult for the timing for her leaving the Dromorne properties was tighter than she had hoped, as Martin's cousin wished to inhabit the family seats before the end of July.

Oh, granted, Martin had left her with enough money to procure another property, but the speed of change was unsettling, all the decisions she needed to make alone daunting and dispiriting.

It was as if the black of her clothes had leaked into her blood, despair and dullness leaving their mark upon her. Taking in a breath, she admonished herself. She had options and possibilities and Florencia, far from being depressed by losing the only man she had known as a father, seemed barely perturbed by his absence.

Eleanor frowned. They had not been as close as she might have hoped. Perhaps Martin's illness had precluded a lot of the joy she had seen in him in Italy, though if she was truthful even there he had been more of a safe man than a happy one.

Safety.

In the throws of change she felt her fingers clench into a fist, the dread that she had woken up with thinking about this visit mounting as the Wellingham town house came into view. If Cristo Wellingham were here, she would turn and leave no matter what explanation might be offered. The very danger of it all sapped what little energy she had left and she swayed.

'Are you all right, my lady?' Patricia, her maid travelling with them, looked concerned, though nothing seemed to faze her daughter, whose whole attention was on the puppies.

'I hope the puppies have not grown too much, Mama. I hope I can hold one and give it a cuddle. Will they let me carry it around, do you think?'

'Shush, child. Can you not see your mother is tired and all these questions are sapping her energy further?'

Florencia's dark eyes came around to hers, the joy in them squashed by criticism.

'I did not mean…'

'No.' Eleanor shook her head. 'It is lovely to see you so excited and I am certain you will be able to hold a puppy if you are careful.'

Her daughter's smile blossomed and in that second she looked so like Cristo Wellingham that Eleanor was frightened.

Would Emerald Wellingham see it? Would the distance the wider family seemed happy to keep her at still stand should others determine the truth?

The Wellinghams were powerful and ruthless and anyone crossing the needs of its members could find themselves with more than a fight on their hands. The wisdom of this visit became less obvious and had they not been outside the front steps Eleanor might have bade the driver to have taken them straight home. But with the door opening and the Duchess walking out with three infants of various ages at her side, she could do nothing but wait as the steps to climb down from the conveyance were put into place.

'It is only us here today, I am afraid, as my husband and his two brothers are at Falder until tomorrow.'

Emerald Wellingham's eyes were warm, an undercurrent of a smile lingering beneath the welcome as her gaze touched on the silver hair of her guest's daughter, suddenly shy in the company of all the children.

'Perhaps Ashton could take your daughter to see the puppies? We have not as yet named them all and the children thought that she might like to help in the process.'

Florencia immediately came out from behind her skirts, the promise of naming a dog more thrilling than even shyness could overcome.

'Mama said that I might hold one…'

'Indeed.' Emerald had bent down, her glance taking in every feature on Florencia's face. 'You are as beautiful as your mother is, my love,' she said after a moment and Eleanor released the breath that she had been holding. Not the comparison that she had been dreading after all. The tight unease in her stomach uncoiled slightly and she watched as her daughter was enfolded by young Wellinghams and led off around the corner of the town house, two maids in tow.

'I have asked for tea to be served in the green salon over-looking the garden,' Emerald Wellingham said. 'The room is one that has always been my favourite and we would be able to hear the children.'

'That sounds lovely.'

Following the Duchess, she saw that the impressive hall opened out into a large room with windows and doors along one whole side facing onto a small garden. The wall opposite was filled with drawings of the wider family and Eleanor's gaze fastened instantly on the ones of Cristo Wellingham.

Emerald must have seen her looking. 'My brother-in-law has recently bought the Graveson property, which lies on the eastern boundary of Falder, and is in the process of having it completely modernised. The house sits near the sea and has always been one of my favourites. I do hope that you might see it some time.'

'If he was there, I should doubt he would wish me any-where near him.' Suddenly Eleanor had had enough of pretence and the interminable drudgery of manners, though surprisingly Emerald laughed.

'You talk of the fiasco with the kidnapping, I presume. I always wondered why you did not speak out in his defence over that?'

'Speak out? But my husband sent word to the constabulary ordering his release.'

'I think it may have been your word Cristo sought, Lady Dromorne.'

Eleanor reddened. Martin had told her Cristo had been relieved to know she did not seek further contact and he had never once tried to see her again, staying out of Bath with all the determination of a man who had long since let go of any other feelings. Even when he had come to offer his condolences and she had squeezed his hand he had merely pulled away while offering shallow words of sympathy.

Not knowing what to do, she placed her teacup on the small side table, taking care not to spill a single drop. 'I am not quite certain what you mean, your Grace.'

'Are you not? Perhaps then there is another drawing you might wish to look at.' She picked up an oval frame from a small table beside her. 'This is of Cristo when he was a young boy of about five. Beatrice found it amongst some books she kept for him whilst he was away.'

With her hands shaking, Eleanor took the velvet-covered frame.

Florencia's face appeared from the faded image, her hair longer and the line of her cheek a little more rounded, but every other feature unmistakably similar.

Eleanor turned the portrait over and placed it down beside her cup of tea. The anger in her was sharp.

'Are you warning me away by showing me this?'

'Oh, I think you have managed to do that all by yourself, Eleanor. In fact it is quite the opposite effect that I am after.'

'I don't understand.'

'I want to give Cristo the chance to get to know his daughter.'

Standing, a dizzy horror consumed Eleanor. 'By taking her from me?'

'It's not retribution I am after, but accord. If the ties that hold you to our family must remain a secret to protect

Florencia, then so be it, but that does not mean the child should know nothing of her Wellingham ancestry.'

The knowledge that Emerald Wellingham was not implying ruin, but rather some form of compromise, fortified Eleanor. The cards were stacked against her, but she needed to give the woman some sense of what had happened before now. She sat down again and lowered her voice. 'I was eighteen when I became pregnant, a young and foolish girl who had no capacity for brandy and a great desire for independence. I made a mistake one night five years ago and your brother-in-law has made it very plain that he desires no further communion with me.'

'Do you love him?'

Eleanor stopped to regroup.

Love. Him.

The ache inside hollowed with the effort of hiding all that she felt and the determination she saw in the Duchess of Carisbrook's turquoise eyes made her pause. It was not condemnation that Eleanor saw, but strength. 'If you do, my advice would be to fight for him.'

'How?' Her heart raced as she enunciated the single word, because in the query she admitted everything.

'The house I told you a friend has to the north-west of London may be the place to begin. You are, after all, a sensible widow with the freedom to travel alone wherever you might wish to. Once there, we could contrive a way to have my brother-in-law visit.'

'Visit?'

'Make what you want of the word. If it were me, I should

be deciding what makes a man stay with a woman and never look further afield.'

A thrill of something forbidden raced through Eleanor's body. Alone with Cristo and in the countryside with no other distractions—would she have the courage to place her heart in his hands? The sheer boldness of the plan was exhilarating. But what if he did not wish to see her, despite all that Emerald Wellingham was saying? And what of Martin, only a week past being buried? Grief and guilt vied with desire and lost.

'Is this house available soon?'

'You just need to say the word and I will send instructions to the housekeeper.'

Cristo paced up and down on the intricate Ausbusson rug in the library at Graveson. It had been almost two weeks since the funeral of Martin Westbury and the anger that ate at him did not seem to be abating in the slightest.

The touch of Eleanor's gloved fingers had ignited all the emotion that he had thought to have discarded. Hell, she had never once tried to contact him and their daughter was growing by the day.

He wished Ashe and Emerald might depart soon, the dinner long since finished and the hour near to eleven, though the thought made him frown. Not too long ago he would have just been beginning his night, the haunts of Paris better after midnight when the true character of the city was revealed. These days he was tired before the clocks struck eight.

'I have a plan to breed horses as you will be doing here

at Graveson, Cris.' Emerald stood and fiddled with an ornament on the mantel and a vague sense of disquiet filled Cristo. Something was not quite as it seemed and he had had enough practice in his life to be certain of a veiled purpose.

'At Falder?'

She turned at that, a look in her eyes that was difficult to interpret. 'No. At Azziz's house in High Wycombe. The hills are rolling and the paddocks are filled with clover and he took quickly to the idea.'

'Sounds ideal.'

Asher laughed. 'You have not spoken about this to me before, Emmie, but Cris and I can take a look at the place if you want. Would you be up to the task, brother?'

Appreciation wreathed Emerald's face, giving the impression that the subject had been closed to her satisfaction, but Cristo, on his part, watched Ashe. Could he not see that his wife was up to something or was he in on the scheme as well? Lord, trust was something that had to be fostered. He downed the brandy in his hand and the scepticism that had dogged him since he was a youth receded a little.

'I saw Eleanor Westbury a week ago by the way, Cristo. She came to our London town house with that lovely little daughter of hers to look at the puppies.' The glass he was about to carefully place on the table landed with a jolt.

'I thought as a family we had decided she should be avoided at all costs, Emmie?' Ashe's question had a thread of irritation in it, heartening Cristo. 'We certainly don't want that whole business of the fiasco at the docks to be raised again in the public mind.'

'It was a quiet meeting at home, my love, and the woman is not as I expected her to be.'

'How would you describe her then?'

'Alone.'

The single word rang around the library, and the fury that had held Cristo ransom began to form into something else.

'Doesn't she have Dromorne's family about her?' He tried to make the query perfunctory.

'The sister and her entourage never even came to the funeral and the cousin wants them out of the house before the end of July. He was always set to inherit the titles, it seems, and by all accounts is a greedy man. Eleanor Westbury's immediate family died years back, so she is truly alone.'

'Lord.'

'She talks of moving to the country and buying an estate. Her child adores animals, it seems. She fell in love with a little black-and-white puppy whilst at the town house and the children allowed her to name it.'

Before he could stop himself Cristo asked the question. 'What did she come up with?'

'Patch. She said he reminded her of a pirate and I could not help but agree to the name.'

'Has the dog found a home yet?'

'No. Are you interested in giving him one?'

Again Cristo felt deception in the air. 'Graveson Manor could do with the presence of a hound. One is as good as another.'

'Then I shall mark him down as yours. He should be ready to take home next week, though I should probably warn you the dog is the runt of the litter and will need a great deal of attention. Have you had a pet before?'

'No.'

That made Asher start. 'Surely you did at Falder, Cris. We all did, for God's sake.'

'Ashborne decided I was not responsible enough to be given authority over an animal and never allowed it.'

Cristo smiled to take the sting away from the hurt. His father had been a man who was distant and reserved at best. When Alice was not there to intervene and when the older boys had gone off to school he had made certain that his bastard son understood exactly the sacrifices he was making to house him.

A by-blow from one moment of madness in a country he had never returned to. Only that! A son he had not had the inclination to truly know. Cristo frowned, thinking of something that had not occurred to him before. Was he doing exactly the same to his own daughter?

His mind raced ahead to the puppy. Florencia had loved it. Perhaps she might find out that it now resided with him and would want to come and visit.

He pushed such fanciful thoughts aside. Eleanor would never allow it.

'Ashborne was a man to seldom show his feelings to anyone, Cris. Taris and I would talk about it often and see the difference with Jack's papa. I can't remember him ever laying a hand on me save in discipline, though Alice would say it was in his nature to be reserved. We were glad to go off to school.'

A chunk of ice fell from Cristo's heart. Just like that. Drip,

drip, drip. For he remembered exactly the same thing. A mantle of guilt dislodged anger.

'I wish you might have said something to me at the time.'

Asher looked at him keenly. 'You thought it was only you he was aloof with?'

Despite meaning not to, he nodded, the many years between his brothers and him compounding the problem. If he had been older they might have said something, included him more. As it was he had had the company of a younger sister and a bunch of wild friends at Eton. No wonder he had taken the track of least resistance. When Ashborne had shouted at him for the next unwise and hare-brained escapade at least he had looked him in the eye and known that he still existed.

Fact skewered fiction. Perhaps it was not the circumstances of his birth after all that had alienated them. Perhaps it was just Ashborne's character that had left a truth unsaid. The softer edge of England reached around him and held him close.

The many lights of Falder could be seen on the hill beside Graveson and in the western horizon the new moon was low and huge.

Home and a place.

And a puppy now. Patch.

He would ask Milne to prepare a bed for the dog to sleep on in the small dressing room off his chamber. He only hoped Patch might effect the sort of joy in his daughter that he had a great wish to see.

* * *

He should not have brought the damn dog! He knew that the moment he had set foot in the carriage for High Wycombe and it had climbed upon his knee with its sad drooping eyes and been sick upon his lap.

A runt was no real description of the physical attributes of this animal and he wondered at his daughter's decision to choose a dog with no thought for its future development. He was the size of a large kitten with a tail that defied gravity and if Emerald still insisted that the family King Charles spaniel had found another of its like then she had to be kidding herself.

This puppy looked like the result of a mongrel from the backstreets of east London taking one very lucky chance.

'Sit still,' he ordered the wriggling hound and was surprised when it did so and fell instantly asleep. He liked the feel of its breath against the back of his hand as the carriage hurled through the last of the countryside towards the house that Emerald's friend Azziz owned.

Chapter Seventeen

'Florencia. Where are you?'

A small giggle alerted Eleanor to the fact that her daughter now hid behind the oak tree at the far end of the garden and she made her way down the line of ill-cut box hedging.

'Is she here? No. Could she be here?' She lifted the leaves of a large plant that drooped across the garden. 'No, not there either.' The giggles began again and the skirt of Florencia's dress was blowing in the wind outside the line of bark.

With a quick dash to the left she caught her daughter to her and swung her round, their hair catching together, undressed and falling long in the slight edge of sun.

It was how Cristo saw them first, laughing and entangled, a mother showing all the affection in the world to a child who plainly loved her. Eleanor was in black, though the lace at her bodice was loose and the swell of her breasts made the colour alluring in a way the pastel shades had never been. His daughter was wreathed in dark blue with a string of what looked to be her mother's pearls draped in a single strand around her neck.

Interest replaced shock, which in its own turn was replaced by wariness. Had Eleanor fashioned this meeting?

When their eyes caught the rose in her cheeks was flushed high.

He stepped forwards and removed his hat, his fingers gripping the fabric so hard he wondered how it did not tear.

'Lady Dromorne?' Florencia lost her smile in the instant of his question and hid in the dark skirts, but Eleanor said nothing, the edges of her lips bound together as though she would not allow even the hint of an answer.

Emerald's evasive dissembling was suddenly explained. She had set this whole thing up and Asher's withdrawal from the trip five minutes before departure meant that he was also in on the plot. Lord, when he returned he would strangle them both. He swore he would.

Right now he needed to at least address the worry he saw so prominently in Eleanor's eyes.

But how?

The wriggling bundle under the jacket of his coat solved the whole problem for, as a small black-and-white head poked out from beneath the lapels of his jacket, he saw in the wide smile on his daughter's face an absolute delight.

She ran forwards, stopping only a foot or so away from him, the silver in her hair whipped by wind and for the first time ever he heard her speak.

'Patch? You brought Patch here?' A small hand reached out to tickle the dog's nose, wonder in her eyes.

'Florencia, this is Lord Cristo Wellingham.'

Cristo's brows were raised, but he did not correct her. Not father, not papa, only a title that a child might or might not remember. The smile looked as fixed on Eleanor's face as it was on his.

'Hello.' He brought out the squirming puppy and held it towards her. She took it immediately, cuddling it in the way only small children can, his pink tongue licking her chin.

When she laughed he saw a child so like him that there could be no possible question of her parentage.

'I love animals.'

He smiled. 'And what else do you love?'

'I am learning to play the piano.'

'Perhaps one day you might play it to me?' He thought of his own Stein sitting at Graveson. It had been so long since he had played anything at all.

Eleanor saw that Florencia was unusually brave, this notice from a stranger overcoming her more normal shyness. Her feet scuffed the ground as the puppy jiggled and she saw Cristo take in the movement, the hunger in his eyes poignant. *I have missed years*, his expression said, *and I am not going to miss another moment.*

'You could show Lord Cristo some of your drawings,' she suggested. The bag Florencia often carried with her lay on the brick steps four feet away and she hurried to get it.

'There is a seat just here.' Eleanor indicated an old bench. 'If you sat on his knee, it might be easier for you both to see, darling.'

Keep it light and easy and natural, Eleanor thought, her hand trembling as she handed her daughter the book. She was pleased when Florencia did as she was asked and stood before him and the look of wonder on Cristo's face as he touched his child so carefully brought mistiness to her eyes.

She made much of doing up the buckle of the bag as he made room for Florencia and the puppy on his lap.

'This is our house,' her daughter said after a moment, 'and this is Papa. He is in Heaven because he likes being there now. This is Sophie in her yellow gown and Margaret in her blue one. They don't live with us any more but they used to. And this is my dog.'

Eleanor craned her neck forward. A black-and-white dog who looked a lot like Patch gambolled on the page.

'The dog she imagines, I'm afraid, as Martin was allergic to any pet hair.'

'And is this you next to your mama? The beautiful girl with the princess locks?'

Florencia laughed and suddenly reached out to his hair, her small fingers threading through the colour. 'Your hair is exactly the same as mine,' she said before returning to the book and flicking the page.

Over their daughter's head Cristo's eyes met hers, a scar she had not seen before marking the skin beneath the left one. The fight on the docks had scarred him and she wished she might have touched it, wished she might have simply leant over and run her finger across the sharp angles in his cheek. But she sat there, listening to the explanations of each page and the interested comments that followed them until the book was finished, a chronicle of everyday life explained away in ink.

'There is a stretch of grass just through those trees. I saw it in the carriage as we came in. Would you ladies like a walk?'

The question was addressed to Eleanor, but it was Florencia who answered.

'Oh, yes, please, Mama. Please let us have a walk. I could take Patch.'

Eleanor weighed up her options.

'Very well, but just for a few moments.' She hated that part in her voice that sounded so stern and tight.

Cristo felt his daughter's hand creep into his own as they made their way through the hedge and into the open ground.

Florencia was small and fragile like Eleanor, but that was where any similarity ended. Her hair and her eyes and the shape of her face were exactly his own and she played the piano as he did. A great weight of love tugged his heart into a different beat and he wished that they might have been truly a family taking in the air before going back home.

When Florencia skipped off to pick a bunch of daisies Eleanor was quick to use the moment.

'I did not ever think that you would travel to High Wycombe.'

'Indeed, Lady Dromorne, I may not have if I had known you to be here. In London when you did not return to help me I promised to forget you. But Emerald asked me to look at the property for her—a ruse on her part to get us together, no doubt.'

'I could not come—'

He broke in. 'Or write or send a messenger? It was only that I needed, Eleanor, and instead there was nothing.'

'I could do none of these things you speak of because

Diana, Martin's sister, kidnapped me and took me up north. She fed me laudanum until a servant who had a brother in our London town house got word to Martin. By then you were free of all charges.'

'Diana kidnapped you?' He could barely take in the truth of what she told him. 'Why would she do that?'

'For her daughters' sake, after I told her that you were Florencia's father. She wanted the family reputation protected against scandal, you see, and thought that was the way to do it.'

'Lord, you could have died. Where the hell is she now?'

'In Scotland. She has promised not to return to London for a very long time.'

The silence between them grew; clearing her throat, Eleanor began uncertainly. 'I realise that Martin came to see you and you made it very clear to him that you did not wish for any further communication between us.'

'Your husband told you that?'

'He did. I understand how very easily I could be an embarrassment to your family, but...'

The words were whipped from her as eyes of ice bored into her own.

'I never gave Martin Westbury such a message. Dromorne said that you blamed me for everything and that you would not risk the life of Florencia again after the débâcle at the docks. He said that you wished me dead with all of your heart. I took that as the truth and withdrew.'

Eleanor shook her head. 'Martin told you that?' The sheer

enormity of such a betrayal was impossible to contemplate. 'I cannot believe that of him…'

'He forbade me visit Bath under oath for as long as you resided there and said you never wanted to set eyes on me again. Given the events that had unfolded with Beraud, I assented. You appeared to enjoy a social life that kept you out till all hours, according to the newssheets, and never once tried to regain contact. It was hard to believe otherwise.'

'He used us both, then.'

As she spoke he saw the girl on the bed at the Château Giraudon, her eyes full of hurt and despair, though when Patch gambolled back to jump at her skirts with his long black-and-white ears blowing in the wind her expression changed.

'The dog was a lovely gift, but we cannot possible accept it, for a cousin of Martin's will take over the Dromorne properties and I have yet to find a new home.'

'Then he can stay with me until you are ready for him.'

She shook her head. 'If the world sees you together with Florencia…'

He stopped her by placing his finger on her lower lip, the wind catching at her hair and throwing the length of chestnut back across her shoulders. For a moment he felt he could not breath with the sheer desire he felt for her, the bodice of her gown tight across breasts he had once fondled and suckled. The ache in his groin had him bring his coat farther across his thighs. God, he was becoming erect in the middle of the day with his daughter not ten feet from them. It was Eleanor who looked away first.

'If people talk of the likeness between you, it will be difficult for all of us.'

He laughed and wished that he hadn't as the line between her eyes deepened.

'You worry too much, Eleanor, and I think already it may be too late for that. Did you think to hide her for ever?'

'No. But I don't want her hurt.'

'I promise that she will not be.'

When he hesitated on the path she did the same, the distance between them lessened by the action. Reaching out his hand, he took her gloveless fingers into his own.

'When was she born?'

Eleanor took in a breath. She had known, of course, that he would ask, that the facts hidden would soon not be and that a father had as much right as a mother to all the small details of childhood.

'On July the first in 1826 in Aix-en-Provence. I travelled there after Paris. After that I went to Florence. Martin had offered help and I took hold of such a chance.'

'Because you could not come to me.'

Not a question, but a rebuke. Of himself. Of his part in all that had happened. For the first time she thought of how young they both had been.

'I needed a safe place, Cristo.'

He glanced up at the use of his name. 'And if you had returned, I would have given you one.'

But she did not let him off so lightly. 'A mansion that was renowned for its debauchery and its licentiousness and a kitchen whose food was counted by the number of brandy bottles lining its shelves? I think in truth that there are better homes for a little girl to be raised in.'

'I'll sell the Château Giraudon and buy a place in London for you. I have other money, too.'

'No, she stays a Westbury until…'

Until you marry me.

Lord, she had so very nearly said it. Her hand came to her mouth and she was silent, though the determination that had kept her going all the way up here and through all the days of waiting for him to follow, began to gel.

The sheer negligence of care made her dizzy.

'Until?' His eyes were as dark as she had ever seen them, the pupils lost in ebony.

'Until I marry again.'

'You have someone in mind?'

'Indeed, I do.'

'That would be a mistake.' The words were ground out before he knew it, his hands at his side clenched into fists. Westbury had been dead for less than a month and already she was lining up a successor? The papers from Bath suddenly came to mind. An Original. The toast of society. He wanted to throw her across his back and take her up to bed, now, without words, their bodies melded into one and for ever joined. He wanted to stay here in this ramshackle house in the little village of High Wycombe, away from everyone and everything.

But he could see in her eyes a misgiving that would need a more careful diplomacy. Changing tack, he came in from another angle.

'Emerald no doubt sent us on such a wild goose chase for a purpose.'

Eleanor blushed and he stepped back.

'Not both of us, then?' He swore beneath his breath at the duplicity.

Eyes the colour of an afternoon summer sky met his. 'The Duchess had guessed about your relationship with Florencia. When she suggested we should at least talk, I could hardly refuse to do so.'

'My town house in London would have been a lot closer.'

'And a lot easier to leave.'

'My carriage is here.'

'Actually it isn't quite where you might think it, though of course I shall ask for it to be returned—'

He didn't let her finish.

'For a woman who has an intended groom waiting in the wings, you are astoundingly careless.'

'A groom?'

'The man you have just told me you have in mind to marry. Do you not think he would take offence at our being alone here?'

Surprisingly she smiled and the dimples in her cheeks were deep. Lord. The broadsheets of Bath had not understated her beauty one little bit. In London she had been swathed in pastels, caution and sorrow. Here, in the open air with her hair down and the generous spill of her bosom over a simple gown of mourning, she was unforgettable.

Cursing, he looked away, though not before he had seen a flicker of satisfaction on her face. The world spun into another angle as he mulled upon it. Could she have meant him to stay here for more than just talk? The magnitude of the plan hardly indicated fainthearted trepidation after all and any woman must have realised the danger inherent in such a proposition.

Alone, together, with the past between them and the present strewn across a need that had never settled.

He wanted her with a plain and utter hunger. Still, there were questions that he needed answers to; seeing that Florencia was a good distance away playing with Patch, he took his chance.

'If I am alone with you in the house tonight, Eleanor, I doubt that I would have the temperance to sleep in a separate bed.'

'Is that a warning, my lord?'

'No, *ma chérie*. It's a certainty.'

Florencia's cry brought their attention to her.

'Look, Mama. Patch is chasing his tail.'

'Just as I am chasing mine,' he murmured to himself and was again confused by Eleanor's returning smile as she slipped from his side to view the puppy's antics with their daughter.

Chapter Eighteen

The room the housekeeper showed him to overlooked the front of the house and was larger than any bedchamber he had ever been in. Divided into two separate spaces, he was interested to see the shape of a piano beneath a large dust-sheet. Pulling it aside, he ascertained the instrument to be a Broadwood and his curiosity quickened. It had been an age since he had sat at a piano and played. Positioning the stool, he placed his fingers over the chords before letting them sink into the keys.

Like coming home. Almost sacrosanct.

As he closed his eyes the first movement of Beethoven's 'Moonlight Sonata' spilled into the room, the waves of tension building and resolving. All the broken cords of his life were in that tune, the hell ship, his father's distance and the loneliness that had kept him bound in France.

His fingers found notes that had never left him. In Paris he had only ever heard the mistakes, but this afternoon in the sunlight under a clear blue sky he heard the music, peaceful, meditative, the harmony and feelings speaking to him.

Eleanor was in the pulse of the rhythm, in the tension and release as the line he created widened into a broad arch, lilting through the silence, hanging across his heart like a banner.

The muscles in his arms quivered, unused to such an exacting toil, but still he did not stop, could not stop, the stormy third movement taking over from the first. Passion and wild accents reigned now, the ferocity of the *sforzando* notes and the fortissimo passages unbridled.

Like Heaven and like a home.

Eleanor.

His fingers paused on the keys as her name loosened anger and he knew for certain, in that one small second of silence, that if he ever lost her he would never be found again.

Listening from the hallway outside the room, Eleanor leaned against the wall with an outright astonishment.

He played the piano as skilfully as she had ever heard anyone do so, even without the little finger on his right hand, the flamboyance of his style suiting the piece with an unquestioned exactness. When had he learned? She remembered the piano in his room at the Château Giraudon, but here in England she hadn't heard even a whisper of his brilliance.

When the last of the notes faded into quiet she walked into the chamber. Cristo sat with his eyes closed and the sun from a wide window on his hair.

'It is good to play again,' he began as if he had known she was there outside all along and there was a softness in the tone of his voice that she had not heard before. His glance now took in every part of her.

'It is a beautiful tune.'

'Beethoven's piano Sonata number fourteen in C-sharp minor. Many call it the "Moonlight Sonata" because legend has it he wrote the piece whilst playing for a blind girl at night.' He hesitated. 'A compelling anecdote, I would imagine.'

'In Bath I went to many piano recitals and, even given my untrained ear, yours sounded more skilled than all of them.'

He laughed. 'Have dinner with me in here and I will play you others.'

Her eyes flickered to the large bed on the far wall, almost on the same proportions as the room, and she blushed.

'Practice makes perfect,' he quipped, the edge of a seriousness in his words contradicting humour as he stood.

Eleanor swallowed. When it actually came to it the whole madness of ever imagining she could seduce such a man seemed most unwise. If she had any sense she would scuttle from this room and hide, but the vision of them both on the bed in the moonlight was startling, like the song he played come to life, exotic, unbridled and passionate.

'I am the father of your daughter…'

And of your son. She almost said it.

'And a man who would never hurt you! Take a chance, my Eleanor. Take a chance on me and live.'

It was if he had read her mind, the years since she had last truly lived filled with greyness. Only one night five years ago, yet she remembered every second as if it were yesterday.

But seduction was more difficult when words were required and the way he was looking at her indicated a definite need for them. Not yet, she thought. Not yet. Clearing her throat, she began uncertainly.

'There are towels in the cupboards and the maid will be up with water for a bath should you wish it.' The domestic details steadied her, made the scene more normal. In the distance she heard Florencia and knew that he had heard her too.

'Dinner will be at eight in the blue salon.'

Pulling the banter back, he answered promptly, 'I shall look forward to it.'

She dressed carefully that night in a dark blue gown that she had put aside for exactly this purpose. Seduction was an art form, after all, and a woman of almost twenty-five with only one night of loving behind her needed all the help she could muster.

She did not wear undergarments and the feel of the silk bodice against bare skin was exciting, her womanhood beating in a throb between her legs.

Anticipation.

Even the perfume she dabbed profusely on parts of her body that she had not before added to the tension.

Her hair she wore unadorned, the length of it spilling across her shoulders and down towards her hips, curling in the damp. She had dismissed her lady's maid for the night to sit in the nursery.

She wished she had the courage to wear nothing. To turn up at the dinner table wearing only stockings and pearls, but a lifetime of caution harboured inside her and she was still not quite certain of his intent.

Could this be just another night for him, just another coupling?

She shook her head firmly, but it was not the action of a woman who would place much weight on warning. No. It was the knowledge of one who finally felt whole and welcomed what might happen next with all her heart and soul.

Cristo Wellingham was the man she had loved from the very first second of meeting him and every other suitor dulled in comparison. In Bath over the last months there had been many who offered more than just a casual friendship, given that Martin never accompanied her to any function whatsoever—men who were honourable and decent and good, but she felt nothing for them. No lack of breath or altered heartbeat. No rush of delight or a thrill of meeting glances. Only one man, even with his distant presence in a house as big as this one, had the ability to affect her.

Tucking back an errant curl, she took one last look in the mirror before she left the room to meet him.

The thin silk of her gown barely covered her and the outline of her nipples could be plainly seen. Beckoning. Cristo felt like simply stepping forwards and ripping the flimsy thing off, but he had travelled that path once before with Eleanor and knew enough to realise this time he needed to leave the power in her hands.

'My lady.' Hard to say with any sense of decorum to a woman dressed as she was.

'My lord.' Manners simmered above pure sensuality. Her lips were deep cherry red. 'I have asked the servants to leave our supper out and dismissed them for the night. I hope you don't mind helping yourself?'

'Indeed, I do not.' He felt his manhood rise another notch with the words so artlessly said, and moved to ease the tightness of his breeches.

The cravat at his neck was strangling, the starched collar rough against the skin at his throat. A hundred pounds of material seemed to hang upon his frame when all she wore was the lightest of gossamer silk.

Her feet were bare. He had seen that in the first second of meeting her, peeping out beneath the hem of her skirt. The scent of gardenias and violets was strong on her skin.

'Florencia…?'

'Is in her room in bed. My maid is watching over her.'

'So it is just us?'

The beginning of a smile played around her lips and he looked around the room to gather his wits. A *chaise longue* in velvet was pushed against the far wall. On the table near the food flowers stood, the urns they were displayed in etched with woodland scenes.

Two heavy carpets lay on the floor, a pile of cushions heaped next to them. Almost accidentally. In the grate at the far end of the room a fire blazed.

'Would you like some wine?' She gestured to a bottle and glasses and he nodded, feeling like a man who had strayed into a pleasure dome, the woman before him a culmination of every young boy's fantasy.

'How much would you like?'

At her words he removed the glass from her fingers, placing it on a table behind her. Up this close he was taller than she remembered him and a lot bigger; the boy she had known in Paris replaced by the man.

'I want as much as you would give me, Eleanor.' His voice broke on her name and he gathered her close, warm breath against her cheeks and the glorious brown of his eyes locked into hers.

'*Ma chérie,*' he said as his lips came down and his hands threaded through her hair, the lover suddenly there again, gentle but firm. She could not have pulled away even had she wanted to.

But she didn't want to.

Opening her mouth easily, he came inside, his tongue finding hers as he slanted his head. Heat and breath and anger mixed with want and love and regret; a recipe matured by time and by memory.

She was eighteen again, and shameless, her need wild beneath cold clear silk and the sharp edge of discovery.

This time she had lured him to her. The power of it was exhilarating, yet still she pulled back and placed her hands upon his chest.

'Not yet, *monseigneur.*' Muscles bunched along the line of his jaw, but he let her go. A gentleman who would not coerce a lady. Smiling, she looked down and saw how very much he wanted her.

'For I wish to undress you first.'

* * *

She was a hundred times more experienced than she had been when he had taken her last and more lethal than any courtesan he'd had the pleasure of since. The regret that it had not been him to teach her surfaced as he stood perfectly still, feeling her fingers at his neck unlacing the cravat, her skin playing havoc against his own. He seldom allowed anyone dominion over his body, but he made himself relax. Beneath his shirt were the scars endured at eighteen, scars he had never willingly shown anyone before, stigma drawn in the opaque ridges of flesh. When her hands began to peel back the linen he froze.

'I generally like to keep it on.'

'Because of the marks upon your back?'

He was irritated by the shame that surfaced, over a decade ago and still having the power to hurt. He was also surprised she had remembered at all.

'You have a good memory.' He tried to keep the tone as light as he could, airy, inconsequential and nonchalant.

'As I have only ever lain with one man it is not a thing easily forgotten.'

'One?' He could not understand what she was telling him.

'Martin was impotent.'

Now he did.

'Lord.' The blue in her eyes had darkened, bruised with truth. 'Lord,' he repeated again. 'So it has only been me?'

'It was why I was out on the town so much in Bath, for he suddenly seemed to want a closer relationship in other ways and I could not give it to him. By staying out late it meant he was always asleep in his room when I returned.'

The world he lived in reshaped into something unrecognisable. Just him. Just her. Throwing off his shirt, he turned so that she could see the marks.

'After Nigel I took passage on a ship run by a captain who thought hurting others was fun. It was a full month before I escaped and for a long time after that...' He stopped because he could not go on.

'You trusted no one?' Eleanor's words were whispered, an understanding in them that made him want to weep.

'If I could go back, I would have trusted you.'

She smiled. 'And if I could go back, I would have knocked on the door of the Château Giraudon and taken up your offer of protection.'

'Over five years...' Three words steeped in remorse.

'But not a day more.'

Her certainty was like a balm and he reached forwards to trace the shape of her cheek before venturing lower, the skin on her neck and the full abundance of breast barely covered in fabric.

Her head fell back and she closed her eyes and he watched her as he found one nipple and turned it between his fingers. Dark blue silk fell away as he cradled the flesh and leant down to suckle.

Relief flooded into the parts of her body that had laid so dormant, his lips and tongue weaving magic.

When she felt the silk tumble from her shoulders she just stood there, in the room with the firelight and candlelight and perfume, a woman who wanted all that would come next and be damned for any consequence. She held his head, the thick glossiness of his hair twisted in her fingers, so that pain lingered in pleasure in the same measure as it rested in his pull on her nipple.

Not quite easy.

Not quite amenable.

No bedroom. No certain privacy. A risk. A gamble. His caresses made her limbs fluid and warm.

She wanted Cristo Wellingham to bury himself inside her with an urgency that was frightening, so when he lifted his head and smiled she was flustered by his restraint.

'Now. Take me now.'

'And have years of waiting to be finished in a few minutes? I think not, my lovely Eleanor.' His teeth were white. 'Your very first time was a rushed affair, but I swear, sweetheart, this time will not be.'

Placing her forefinger in his mouth, he rolled it on his tongue, in and out, spread across wetness, deep and deeper. The room tilted as his free hand found the fabric of her skirt, bunching it up around her bottom before entering the hidden folds. One finger and then two, the penetration the same as those at her mouth.

Her breath simply ceased. She swore it did, the cold silk, the moonlight on the carpet, the spills of ecstasy linked by feeling at both ends of her body.

Until he stopped.

'Not yet, my love. Not yet.'

Leading her to the *chaise longue*, he sat her down, the

midnight silk beneath her breasts. When her nipples tightened in the cool air he handed her a glass of wine.

Red like blood. Symbolic somehow. Stained in the burst of grape and in the momentary release of perfection.

The outline of his manhood was fierce in its shape behind tight breeches and she could barely believe that this was not a dream, that it was real and that he had called her his sweetheart.

When her more usual prudence deserted her completely, she reached forwards to lay her hands upon his groin.

He groaned and the smile on his face was pained. Perhaps he would not enjoy that caress, she thought, her fingers dropping back into her lap.

'Martin Westbury must have had ice in his veins to be impotent with you.'

She shook her head. 'When he found me in Aix I was very ill. He saved my life by taking me to Italy. After that it was hard to leave him.'

'Ill…?'

'From childbirth.' She turned her face away so that he might not see what was in her expression, but he was adept at picking up the nuances and turned it back.

'You are not telling me everything.'

She breathed in once and then twice, and his fingers found her own, like a lifeline in a swirling sea, she was to think later, though when she did not speak he began with a story.

'My mother was Sylvienne de Caviglione. She met my father a month before she was to be married off in an effort to secure a political alliance. Sylvienne had hoped for a younger husband and Ashborne was a long way from home and lonely. When the result of their indiscretion was known she was sent to the country. I arrived eight and a half months later and my entry into the world was her exit from it. I tell you this, Eleanor, because I do not want any more secrets between us and I can see them in your eyes.'

'Yet you grew up a Wellingham at Falder?'

'My French grandfather had as little use for a bastard as he did for a dead daughter. He sent me to England as fast as he could, though his wife harboured her own measure of guilt and left me her family château in Paris when her husband died. I had killed their only daughter, you see...'

'You blame yourself for your mother's death?'

'She was young and it was a difficult birth.' Fury underlined each word.

'Mothers die in birth as easily as children do.' Eleanor held her other hand rigidly against her side, gripped into a fist.

Now. Now. Tell him now.

She made herself unclench her fingers one by one by one. 'There is a story that says the stars house the souls of the ones who have departed, and that at night, between the autumn equinox and the winter solstice, in the cluster known as the Pleiades, you can see them, and speak to them.'

'Pleiades?'

'The seven stars that sit in the constellation of Taurus.'

She looked across to the window, but only out of habit, for the time of the year was far too early. Still out of caution she did not tell him, did not speak of the times when she

had watched month by month for something meant only
for her.

'Paris watches me from there.'

Tears welled in her eyes unbidden. Her son. Their son.
Missing, and so very far from home. It was good to say his
name out loud and to someone who might have loved him
as much as she did.

Something was wrong. Something hidden and important. Paris? The city? Why would she cry for that? A name,
then?

'Paris?' He repeated the word and she looked up and
nodded. 'Who is Paris, Eleanor?'

The darkness in her blue eyes was like a blanket of dull
pain, stale grief and anger. 'Our Paris. Our son. He lies in
Aix in the cemetery under a marker of white stone.'

The truth of what she said made his heart stop and the
pit of his stomach lurch.

'Another child? There was another child?'

She nodded. 'Florencia had a twin. A brother.' Tears ran
down her cheeks like two rivers, but she did nothing to dash
them away. 'You were not there, so I called him Paris. It was
all I could think of to link him with you.'

'God, Eleanor.' He pulled her to him, as if in the embrace
he might take some of her hurt, some of the suffering as he
imagined how it must have been. Eighteen and alone in a
foreign land with one living baby and one dead one!

'He w-was too tiny. He w-was much t-too tiny. He would
n-not have lived here, either, I d-do not th-think.'

Cristo nodded his head in agreement, not trusting himself to speak.

'And it w-was too soon for them to c-come. Not quite eight months. Florencia was b-bigger. I wanted Paris to live, but h-he didn't.'

The sobs increased, but her head was now nodding up and down, the arms that held him tightening.

In the firelight and in a strange house, miles from London, it seemed as if it were only them left in the whole wide world as she cried out her many years of silence.

Chapter Nineteen

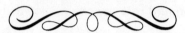

She woke up in his bed. A blanket had been pulled over her and a pillow tucked beneath her head. It was still dark, though a small candle on the mantel had burnt down almost to the plate, making her calculate that many hours had passed.

She had told him!

Her hand went to her mouth and she held it there. The evening had begun with seduction in mind and ended in her being asleep, alone and dressed upon his bed and confessing a confidence that she had told no one before. She smiled, for the relief of sharing her secret had eased the burden in a way she could never have imagined.

Footsteps coming towards the room had her sitting up and Cristo appeared a second or so later with a tray. A teapot and two cups sat to one side of a jug of milk.

He had pulled on his shirt, but it was unbuttoned and like her he wore no shoes at all.

'I thought you might be thirsty.'

A flower sat alongside the cups, newly picked, the dew on it magnifying the red.

He handed the perfect bloom to her, candlelight on the bronze of his chest, each muscle well defined.

'It was by itself amongst the weeds when I stepped outside the kitchen door to take in some air. It reminded me of you.'

Smiling, she took his gift and noticed that all of the thorns had been taken off the smooth green stem. When she bent her head to the petals the perfume was of a soft freshness.

Placing the tray on the table, he drew forth a chair from under the window. His knees framed hers now and he looked as if he was searching for just the right thing to say.

'I own land next to Falder. On it stands a manor house named Graveson Manor and it overlooks Return Home Bay. It is beautiful land, Eleanor, with the sea rolling in and the green of fields and trees.' His left hand raked through his untidy blond hair, pushing it back.

The very words made the world a wondrous place, though she sobered when she thought of the path that he was leading her down.

'I could not be your mistress.'

The shock in his dark brown eyes was easily seen. 'It is not as a concubine I want you, Eleanor, but as a wife.'

Her mouth simply dropped open. 'You are asking me to marry you?'

'I am. I hope the groom you had in mind will bow out gracefully.'

She began to laugh. 'It was you I was thinking of. No one else.'

He joined in her humour by smiling broadly. 'I cannot believe that something is finally easy for us. You will marry me and become my wife?'

When she nodded again he stripped the gold ring from his little finger and reached forwards. 'I know it is old-fashioned, but it was the only thing of Alice's that I have. She took it off her finger the night before I left England all those years ago and made me promise it would go to the woman I married.'

'You never wore this in Paris?'

'It was too special. All the others were for show and for the part I was playing of a dissolute and unrestrained lord.'

Joy welled inside her. Special. Her finger ran across the red in the ruby and around the band of gold.

'We will be married with all the family present, because I need to do this properly. As properly as everything so far between us has not been. I cannot wait a year, Eleanor, for your mourning period to be over, so perhaps we could repair to the Continent. Florencia will have a family with cousins and aunts and uncles.'

Her euphoria died down a little. No mention of love, but all of duty.

As he picked up on her uncertainty he dropped her hand, one eye on the door and the other on his watch. He wanted to be gone, from the room, from her and from the promise he had just made. She could see it so very plainly in his face.

Her fingers closed around the golden ring as she wondered if he might ask her to rescind her promise. But he was a Wellingham and responsibility sat on his shoulder as a heavy load. He would do his best by her.

When he leant down and kissed her on the forehead, she was almost reminded of Martin.

'Thank you, Eleanor. You will not regret this decision.'

He had handled that as badly as he had ever handled anything in his life, he thought, as he regained his upstairs chamber, but the raging lust in him was a terrible reminder of how he had hurt her last time. This time he wanted everything perfect. Not rushed or illegal or sordid. Eleanor deserved the very best from him and he was going to give it to her, no expense spared. If he had stayed for even a moment longer with the promises between them, he doubted he could have remained so controlled.

Closing his eyes, he felt the line of his jaw tremble with desperation, his open hands balanced against the wall behind him.

He loved her. He loved her bravery and her honesty and the way she had held him as she cried her heart out. Him, the man who had been the cause of everything in her life that had been difficult.

Forgiveness. He deserved none of it and she might still refuse him. A lump formed in his throat.

If he lost her… He shook his head.

If he even touched her… He shook it again, not trusting the need that he was consumed with.

A board on the stairwell creaked and he swallowed back pity. The material at his groin strained tight as Eleanor came into the room.

With her cheeks blushing pink he thought he had never seen her look more beautiful and the danger of his wretched urgency mounted.

'You should return to your bedroom, Eleanor.' He grimaced at the harshness in his tone, but it was all he could do to stand there and not ravish her as every single particle in his body wanted to.

She held her palm out towards him, the gold of Alice's ring glinting in what little there was left of the firelight.

'I have endured one marriage that was not a love match. I do not think that I could endure another one.' Her voice trembled, but she went on. 'Especially when I know that my heart would be completely broken.'

'I don't understand.'

'I love you, Cristo. I have loved you from our first night together and through all our years of separation. It has only ever been you.'

'Lord.' He stepped forwards. 'There aren't many things I've done right in my life, sweetheart, but having your love is one of them.' He didn't move a muscle but, looking into her eyes, he kept talking so that she might see his honesty.

> *"I brought a heart into the room*
> *But from the room I carried none with me."*

'John Donne?'

When he nodded Eleanor smiled. 'So it was not only for Florencia's sake that you wished for us to be betrothed.'

'You thought that?'

'You left so quickly.'

He grimaced. 'I didn't trust what I might do if I stayed.'

Walking straight into his arms. she turned her face up to his. 'I love you.'

'I love you, too. *Tout se pardonne quand on aime.*'

Where there is love there is forgiveness.

She found him in the silence, the strength of him and the gentleness, a man fully aroused, but trying to show his patience and temperance.

'There are only a few hours left until the dawn, Cristo. Why waste them?'

'You are saying that you should not wish to?'

'I am.'

He pushed down the sleeves on her gown and undid the buttons left at the back. When the blue silk pooled at her feet she was full of neither shyness nor regret.

'I thought you would want everything perfect after the last time.'

'It is,' she replied. 'It is perfect because I have you.'

Much later they lay naked against each other, a blanket pulled across them against the gathering dawn and Cristo's fingers tracing shapes of a heart across her back.

'I think Martin felt the kind of hatred for you that he had never felt about anyone before.' Her hand laid out flat against his chest, her fingers splayed across his heart. 'He was a good man who made a bad choice, but I think had he known what I truly thought about you he would have tried to mend it.'

'You do?' She could hear the doubt in his voice.

He brought her close and she could feel his tongue against

her shoulder and then her neck, the flare of affection almost making her forget how to breathe, but she had another question to ask him.

'Who were the people who kidnapped us?'

He took a moment to answer. 'Colleagues from Paris.'

'Colleagues?'

'I worked as a gatherer of information for England and the Foreign Office and Beraud worked for the Secret Police in France. Sometimes his loyalties incorporated the selling of secrets, for substantial amounts of cash, you understand.'

'You are saying that he would betray his own country?'

'All patriots have their price, and a gambling addiction could not have been easy to manage on the wages Fouche offered.'

'Did you have a price?'

He merely shook his head.

'How did they know about us?'

'By chance. He must have seen us together in London and saw a way to make some money on the side.'

'And Milne?'

'Is completely trustworthy.'

'Are there others who might harm us?'

'If there are, I will make certain that they never come close enough.'

The amber in his eyes darkened and there was a menace in his voice that she absolutely believed. The recognition of an agent of death was chilling.

'But your work with the Foreign Office is finished?'

'It was completed when I left Paris and I have had no

contact since. With you there is something returning that I have not felt in a very long while.'

'What?'

'Joy.'

She laughed.

'There. That is the joy I speak of.'

She laughed again, and the release of gaiety felt like an opiate.

With Cristo and Florencia as her family and the memory of Paris between them, Eleanor felt she could do anything, be anyone, the reckless force of her youth returning in a great and wonderful measure.

'I love you so much, Cristo, that I am sometimes scared because it seems too perfect.'

'After all we have been through perhaps perfect is what we deserve.'

Leaning over, he rifled through a pocket in his jacket and, when he opened his palm, her grandfather's lost medallion lay upon it.

'You kept it?'

The gilded upstairs room in the Château Giraudon seemed close as he wound her hair around his finger. 'It was all that I had left of you. If only I had been wiser then—'

She stopped him simply by slipping the chain around his neck and the warmth between them grew. 'Now is what we do have, Cristo.' The gold glimmered warm in the light.

'I love you, my Eleanor, and I will never let you go.'

'Promise.'

'I do.'

* * *

In the early light of dawn they spoke again of the past.

'I always wondered what was in the letter you brought to Paris from your grandfather,' he said, looking at the sky outside. 'When you left I tossed the sheets from the bed into the fire and the message was lost completely.'

'I never read it, but I presumed it to be about my Uncle Nigel. My uncle had written a confession in the family Bible, you see, all about his part in my brother's death, though I don't think he meant to kill him. He took to the bottle straight after and Grandfather was probably trying to make amends.'

'And because of it I harmed you.'

'Found me.' She turned to watch him. 'Besides, you had to run from England for a mistake that was not in any way your fault.'

'I was always running from mistakes as a youth. The only damn thing I have ever done right is to find you.'

She ran her fingers along the side of his cheek, liking the way he leaned into her touch, his hair silver against her hand.

'You look like an angel, Cristo.'

At that he did laugh. 'And one with very impure thoughts.'

'My angel,' she whispered as his mouth came down full against her own.

Epilogue

Aix-en-Provence, France

Six weeks later Eleanor wore a dress of the lightest yellow to be married in, because the colour suited her mood exactly and because Cristo said that whenever he saw her it was as if the sun had come out.

Her groom wore a jacket of dark blue cloth, his waistcoat embroidered with the Wellingham crest.

Florencia wore gold and so did her cousins, the numerous little bridesmaids and pageboys making a line around her. Even the weather cooperated as they stood to one side of the small chapel, a row of cypress trees sheltering them from the light breeze.

Cristo had leased a beautiful country villa with blue shutters and expansive gardens for the Wellingham party and the wedding took place on the third day after they had arrived in the town where Paris had been buried all those years ago.

She could see his headstone from where she stood beside

the front steps of the chapel, white marble newly carved with all the love and pride befitting a cherished first born.

Smiling, Eleanor tipped her head in her son's direction and with Beatrice-Maude on one side of her and Emerald and Lucinda on the other, she thought that she had never felt quite like this.

Young. Free. Alive. In exactly the place that she should be!

The beginning of a life that stretched on into the years before them. She could barely stand still with the promise of it.

'Well, now,' Beatrice said, her eyes alight with mischief. 'All three of the Wellingham brothers are now most satisfactorily married.'

Emerald cleared her throat. 'But we have one wedding still to go, Lucinda.'

Cristo's sister was careful in her reply. 'I have long since given up on finding a man who lives up to all my expectations, Emmie.'

'Cristo might have said the same, Lucy, but when love comes it takes no mind of what has been or of what is to come. It only focuses on the now.'

As if on cue the men joined them, the pin of gold on the lapel of Cristo's jacket catching the sun: a gift from the French side of his family when they had stopped in Paris to make peace with the past.

She felt his fingers slide into hers, one tracing the ring on her left hand.

Semper veritas—Always truth—engraved in the fine gold.

Placing her other hand across the flat of her stomach, she

knew another truth, and when she caught the turquoise eyes of her sister-in-law upon the gesture, knew that she felt it, too.

A full circle. Like the seasons. A time to be born and a time to die.

Paris. Florencia. And now this child.

With the French sun overhead and her husband and children beside her, Eleanor knew that she, too, had finally come home.

HISTORICAL

Novels coming in May 2011

GLORY AND THE RAKE
Deborah Simmons

As if the continual vandalism of the spa she's renovating weren't enough for Glory Sutton, she also has to deal with the enigmatic Duke of Westfield! As they get drawn into the mystery, they must reveal their own secrets in order to uncover the truth…

LADY DRUSILLA'S ROAD TO RUIN
Christine Merrill

When her flighty sister elopes, Lady Drusilla Rudney knows she has to stop her! She employs the help of ex-army captain John Hendricks. Drusilla's unconventional ways make him want to forget his gentlemanly conduct…and create a scandal of their own!

TO MARRY A MATCHMAKER
Michelle Styles

Lady Henrietta Thorndike hides her lonely heart behind playing Cupid—but Robert Montemorcy knows it has to stop! He bets Henri that she won't be able to resist meddling…only to lose his own heart into the bargain!

THE MERCENARY'S BRIDE
Terri Brisbin

Awarded the title and lands of Thaxted, Brice Fitzwilliam waits to claim his promised bride, but Gillian of Thaxted will *not* submit to the conquering knight! Will Brice risk exposing the chink in his armour by succumbing to the charms of his new wife?

MILLS & BOON

HISTORICAL

**Another exciting novel available
this month:**

SECRET LIFE OF A SCANDALOUS DEBUTANTE

Bronwyn Scott

Just another dull debutante?

From boxing at Jackson's to dancing starry-eyed society belles around London's ballrooms, Beldon Stratten is the perfect English gentleman. And he's looking for a perfectly bland, respectable wife.

Appearances can be deceiving . . .

Exotic Lilya Stefanov is anything but bland. Beldon is intrigued to see the ragamuffin girl he once knew has matured into an elegant lady, poised and polite!

But beneath the mysterious beauty's evening gowns and polished etiquette lies a dangerous secret—and a scandalous sensuality…

HISTORICAL

Another exciting novel available this month:

PIRATE'S DAUGHTER, REBEL WIFE

June Francis

Woman Overboard!

Bridget McDonald is in fear for her life—and her virtue—on board a slave ship. She'd rather take her chances in the ocean's murky depths…

Having plunged over the side, she's rescued by rugged Captain Henry Mariner. Realising Bridget's alone and vulnerable, Harry has good reason to feel guilty about her precarious predicament. Despite her reserve towards him, he knows there is no other option…

The only way to protect her is to marry her!

MILLS & BOON